*A
Harlequin
Romance*

TELL ME MY FORTUNE

OTHER
Harlequin Romances
by MARY BURCHELL

TELL ME MY FORTUNE

by

MARY BURCHELL

HARLEQUIN BOOKS   TORONTO
WINNIPEG

CHAPTER ONE

"SOMETIMES," remarked Katherine, regarding herself in the drawing-room mirror with something between satisfaction and regret, "sometimes I can't help reflecting how extraordinarily useless I am, and it depresses me. Then I think how decorative I am, and it seems to even things up a bit, so I suppose it's all right."

"Extraordinarily illogical reasoning," replied her brother Morley, from the wheeled chair to which he had been condemned ever since a car crash some time before. "But, in any case, there is always Great-Aunt Tabitha. Why, after all, should you toil usefully but revoltingly when, by the thoughtful dispensation of Providence, we have a Great-Aunt Tabitha whose large and solid fortune will inevitably come to us round about the time our papa has finished living on his own diminishing capital?"

"But we can't be absolutely sure about Great-Aunt Tabitha dying at the right moment," put in Alma, with all the cheerful and unmalicious callousness of twelve years. "Someone in the reign of James the First lived to be a hundred and twenty."

"This," Morley pointed out unanswerably, "is not the reign of James the First." And Alma sucked her under-lip and thought again.

"Still——" Leslie, the second daughter, spoke rather soberly. "I know what Kate and Alma mean. It doesn't seem quite decent to plan one's life entirely on the prospect of someone else dying. Even," she added apologetically, "if one has never seen that person."

Her brother, however, brushed that aside easily.

"Decency, my pet, is a question of geography and history," he reminded her. "Transport someone in the normal beachwear of Honolulu to the drawing-room of Queen Victoria, and you have a case of gross indecency. But by the same token—or, probably, a rather different one, now I come to think of it—among certain

7

savage tribes, I don't doubt that to bank on Great-Aunt Tabitha's decease, or even to hasten it, would be considered not only perfectly decent, but even desirable."

"We aren't a savage tribe, though," objected Alma, who liked to bear her part in any family discussion.

"There have been times," Morley replied, "not unconnected with your own activities, when that has been open to doubt."

The others laughed, and Katherine, blinking her gold-tipped lashes, and running an absent hand over her fantastically beautiful chestnut hair, said reflectively,

"I don't know quite what started me on such an uncomfortable topic."

Morley grinned at her.

"I do. You probably heard Father telling Mother that the quarterly bills, like all other quarterly bills before them, were larger than ever, and that starvation stared us in the face and we should all have to retire to the two rooms over the stables if we continued to live at our present rate. Or whatever new flight of fancy his immediate annoyance prompted him to."

"What do you mean by flights of fancy?" demanded Alma, regarding her brother severely, though she adored him. "Don't you believe what Father says? D'you think he tells *lies* about his money?"

"What have we ever done," enquired Morley resignedly, of no one in particular, "to have this dreadfully literal-minded child thrust into the bosom of our unrealistic family? No, Alma, of course I don't think Father tells lies. Or, if I do, I didn't mean to convey that impression. But, like most people who live beyond their incomes, he frequently indulges in financial prophecy—of the most sanguine where his own wishes are concerned, and of the gloomiest when it comes to supplying the wants of someone else."

"I don't know what you're talking about, and I don't believe you do either," asserted Alma. "And, anyway, I hope Katherine's only speaking for herself when she talks about being useless. *I* work hard enough at school, goodness knows!"

8

"But with what result?" enquired her brother unfairly. "With what result?"

"And Leslie isn't useless either," pursued Alma, refusing to be drawn on the awkward subject of school results.

"No." Morley cast a half-humorous, half-affectionate glance at his second sister, who was sitting in a low chair, sewing, with an industry which certainly lent colour to Alma's claim for her. "No, Leslie really isn't a useless person although, according to Katherine's argument, she is sufficiently decorative to warrant her being so. If we were all cast away on a desert island—which Heaven and Great-Aunt Tabitha forbid—Leslie is, of course, the one who would discover edible and nourishing shell-fish nestling among the rocks, a spring of fresh water conveniently near at hand, and some method of weaving the surrounding vegetation into shelter for the night."

"All of which simply means," Leslie said, smiling but not looking up, "that a passion for home comforts is stronger in me than in the rest of you, and I should therefore hustle around in search of them while you were still lying on the beach thinking things over."

Though few might have recognized the fact, probably the most unfortunate thing ever to happen to Richard Greeve was to be left, on his father's death, with a comfortable fortune over which he had complete control.

He was already married at the time to the pretty, affectionate wife who had passed on her dark eyes and her flawless complexion to each one of her four children, and she had certainly not been the one to provide him with a sensible purpose in life, still less to curb his extravagant tendencies.

Indeed, she belonged to that fast disappearing race of women—the attractively helpless. And, like the chameleon, she took her "colour" and character from her surroundings.

If her husband had happened to be a big, commonsense, practical creature, she would probably have clung to him, but been a reasonably practical and common-sense partner. As it was, however, her husband was a big, handsome, unpractical creature, with flamboyant ideas and extravagant notions. And she fluttered happily in the bright, ephemeral world which he created for her, adoring him for his often spectacular follies, and encouraging him just when he needed a little tactful restraint.

Whenever Leslie queried their position—which she had done occasionally since she had come to understand the essential insecurity of it—her mother would assume a sweet, vague, but curiously obstinate expression, and say,

"It's difficult for women to understand these things, dear. Your father must know best. It stands to reason."

She would also add, like Morley—indeed like all of them in moments of crisis over the years,

"And there's always Great-Aunt Tabitha."

For as long as the younger Greeves could remember anything, Great-Aunt Tabitha had been an almost legendary figure in their lives. Incredibly, she had survived to the age of ninety-six, living in a magnificent villa near Biarritz, from which, it appeared, neither invader nor liberator had been able to eject her.

Indisputably, she was one of the few really wealthy people left in that part of Europe, for her husband—a fabulously shrewd merchant who had died at least fifty years before—had invested his fortune so cleverly and in such various concerns that not famine, pestilence nor wars appeared to alter Great-Aunt Tabitha's income to any appreciable degree. Or, at least, so the family legend went.

Richard Greeve was her heir, for he and his children were her sole blood relations. And on his own diminishing capital and the golden prospects of hers had he existed for the last twenty-five years.

On this particular afternoon, when the young Greeves were all gathered in the long drawing-room, lazily pursuing the discussion which Katherine's remark had prompted, it was hard to imagine that drama could hover anywhere near their lives.

The room in which they were, with its gracious proportions, its mellow tints of brown and soft gold and green, its long, beautiful windows, looking on a flower-garden and lawn, at the foot of which a little stream bubbled—this was hardly the setting for drama. And the young things idling there, in their youth and their beauty and their confidence, might have seemed to the fanciful like beings who inhabited some tranquil world where it was always afternoon, and where one was completely and safely insulated from the shocks and trials of everyday life.

Katherine was, perhaps, the supremely beautiful one of the family, with her chestnut hair, her velvety brown eyes and her almost apricot-hued complexion. But Morley was extraordinarily handsome in his thin way, and Alma, though given to ruminating in a slightly cow-like manner when any thought possessed her completely, was a good-looking child.

Leslie was the least obviously beautiful. She had the same velvet brown eyes as the others, with the same curious gold-tipped lashes. But her hair, which was soft and fair and cut rather long, lacked the dramatic colouring of the others, and her complexion, though palely beautiful, was almost colourless beside the gorgeous tints of Katherine's.

She had, however, an admirably proportioned forehead and very beautifully set eyes, which combined to give her glance an essential candour and openness that was sweet and endearing, and, at the same time, carried with it a promise of extreme reliability.

They made a charming picture, scattered about the gracious, faintly shabby room. But, as the door opened and their father came in, they immediately became, not a picture in themselves, but merely the background to a portrait.

Richard Greeve, now nearing sixty, was still good-looking in a rather florid, obvious way, but that was not the quality about him which arrested immediate atten-

11

tion. What made him the unquestioned centre of the scene—any scene, was his absolute and unshakable conviction that this was his position by right.

He was a big man, with a splendid, organ-like speaking voice, on which he played with a shameless, but most effective, virtuosity. In a selfish way, he was extremely fond of his family who, in looks at least, did him great credit. But it is doubtful if he would have been either a kind or an understanding parent to any child who could not add some distinction to his own role as head of the house.

He was being very much head of the house at the moment. Indeed, he addressed them—commandingly, and in a manner which gathered everyone's attention to him instantaneously—as "Children."

It was a term which could hardly be applied with accuracy to any of them except Alma, but it was uttered with such conviction that no one could have dreamed of querying it.

"Children," Richard Greeve said, in the tone of one opening Parliament at a solemn moment in the country's history, "I have news for you."

"Good or bad?" interjected Alma quickly, instinctively sensing a peroration and anxious to settle that point before her father embarked on what he had to say.

She received a quelling glance which told even her that her intrusion was ill-judged.

"In one sense it is sad news," her father conceded, and Morley declared afterwards that he bowed his head as he said this, "for death, though splendid, is always sad. But it is news for which we have been prepared a long time, and which will make a great difference in the lives of all of us. It is, I might say, momentous news. Your Great-Aunt Tabitha is dead."

"At last? I mean, oh, dear!" Katherine flushed at her unfortunate choice of exclamation. "We—we were just talking about her when you came in," she added, obviously with some faint feeling of guilt.

"Then we're all rich now," said Alma crudely and with no saving expression of regret.

"That, my dear, is not the most suitable comment to make upon your Great-Aunt's death," her father told her reprovingly. But Morley said indulgently,

"Well, Father, we've been expecting this most of our lives, you know, and it isn't as though we've ever seen the old lady. Besides," he added reflectively, "I dare say, come to that, one isn't unwilling to go, at ninety-six."

"Are you going over to France for the funeral, Father?" enquired Leslie hastily, hoping to distract his attention from Morley's ill-chosen remarks.

But her choice of distraction was not a happy one, it seemed, for her father frowned.

"Unfortunately, no. Although I should certainly have wished to pay my last respects to Tabitha, the opportunity has been denied me. I learn, to my extreme annoyance, that the funeral has already taken place—before I had even been informed of her death. An extremely disrespectful and high-handed way of doing things, and one for which I hold her legal advisers greatly to blame."

"But they couldn't have advised her about her own funeral," protested Alma, who had been following all this very closely. "It'd be too late, you know."

Richard Greeve looked at his youngest child with a certain lack of favour.

"I am assuming that, in accordance with the usual custom when no immediate relative of the deceased is available, her legal advisers took over the duties"—his voice dropped a couple of notes—"the sad duties—of arranging the funeral and informing the relations. My quarrel with them is that they should have attended to these matters in the wrong order. *I* should have been informed immediately, and I should then have flown over to make suitable arrangements."

"But don't forget the cousin, dear." Mrs. Greeve, who had slipped into the room almost unnoticed and now stood rather like a beautiful wraith beside her husband, softly entered the discussion. "The cousin probably attended to everything."

13

"Then he greatly exceeded his rights and position," retorted her husband firmly. "What is he, anyway?" The question was evidently rhetorical as well as contemptuous, because he proceeded to answer it himself immediately. "Merely a third, fourth or fifth cousin by marriage. Some hanger-on—some remote connection of poor Tabitha's late husband. My Uncle Leopold," he added, in case anyone was getting mixed about relationships.

"But I didn't know there was any cousin," exclaimed Leslie, with interest. "I didn't know Great-Aunt Tabitha had any relations except us."

"One would hardly count so remote a connection as a relation, my dear," her father said, smiling faintly and scornfully. "And by marriage, too," he added, as though marriage were a dishonourable state. Though, in point of fact, he had a great and solemn regard for the bond.

"He must be very, very old, if he's a cousin of Great-Aunt Tabitha," Alma said thoughtfully.

"He seems to feel young enough to undertake the journey to England," Mrs. Greeve said doubtfully.

"In any case, cousinships are such queer things when you begin to get into the third and fourth dimension," Morley pointed out. "I never can remember if second-cousins are the children of first cousins, or whether the children of one are second cousins to the original cousin and third cousins to the children."

"Say that again, slowly," Alma begged, concentrating almost audibly.

But her sisters cried, "Oh, no!" in chorus, and Leslie added,

"What did you say about this cousin coming to England, Mother? You said he felt young enough to undertake the journey. Here, do you mean?"

"Yes." Her mother nodded. "He proposes to come here, to Cranley Magna. He wants to make our acquaintance. I thought"—she glanced doubtfully at her husband—"it was rather nice and friendly of him."

"Did you, my dear?" said her husband with deceptive mildness. "Personally, I asked myself if he were not merely following Tabitha's money to England. But perhaps I am of a nasty, suspicious nature." And he gave a beautiful bass-baritone laugh which invited everyone else to join in mirth over such a preposterous suggestion.

"Perhaps," said Alma, and the moment lost much of its value.

"When is this old man coming?" enquired Katherine.

"Within the next few days, I imagine. I must speak to Mrs. Speers about having a room ready," murmured Mrs. Greeve. And, with a faint, sweet smile round on her family, she drifted out of the room again, in search of her very efficient housekeeper.

Almost immediately her husband followed her, for one of the simple and really endearing things about him was that, although he might pontificate and bluster in her presence, he thought her the loveliest thing in the world, and was never happy long away from her. One could forgive him much for that, Leslie had often thought.

Left to themselves once more, the young Greeves broke into animated discussion. All except Morley, that is to say, who leant back in his chair once more and listened amusedly to what his sisters had to say.

"This really is going to make a difference to us, as Father says," Katherine observed. "Being really rich is quite a different thing from merely having prospects, however good. I wonder if Father will let me go to Italy now and study?" For Katherine had singing ambitions, though so far of a rather dilettante quality.

"Curb your notions of our probable worth, my pet," Morley advised her. "The money comes to Father and, by the time he has taken toll of it for what I trust will be a very long life, we shall probably all have to turn to and earn our own living in advanced middle-age."

"You do think of the most *disgusting* things," declared Alma, giving her brother a small thump. "And, anyway, I mean to be married long before I'm middle-aged."

15

"Opportunity is a fine thing, as the offensive old saying has it," Morley reminded her.

At this, however, Alma looked scornful and said, "I should *make* an opportunity, stoopid."

"I wonder how long this old cousin of Aunt Tabitha's will stay," exclaimed Katherine, who had been following her own thoughts all this time. "Maybe Father is right, and he just wants to park himself here."

"Then, after a suitable interval, during which all the demands of hospitality will have been scrupulously fulfilled, Father will hang out an unmistakable 'no parking' sign, and he will have to go," Morley replied.

"Poor old man," said Alma, with what they all felt to be exaggerated and possibly unnecessary sympathy.

"Anyway, I've already told you, he won't necessarily be an old man," Morley declared. "He may be young and handsome, and fall in love with Kate and marry her."

"Why me?" Katherine wanted to know.

"Because you're the prettiest, I suppose," her brother said. "Anyway, I have an idea it wouldn't be any good his falling in love with Leslie, and Alma is a bit young."

"Why wouldn't it——" began Alma.

But Leslie tossed aside her needlework and interrupted firmly.

"I'll leave you to your romantic planning," she said, her colour just a little high. "I'm going to the village to get some ribbon and other odds and ends. Anyone else coming?"

No one else was coming, it seemed. And without bothering to fetch either a hat or coat, for it was a beautiful, golden August, afternoon, Leslie stepped out of one of the long windows, which served, as did most of the windows in that room, as a garden door, and crossed the lawn to a wicket gate almost hidden in flowering bushes.

She was not at all sorry to be alone. She liked her own company, especially on an afternoon of such absorbing loveliness, and her father's news had provided enough food for thought—inevitably pleasant and speculative

16

thought—without the need for conversation.

She walked slowly, thinking first of the legendary old lady who had just died—with that faintly remorseful, impersonal regret which is all that any of us can achieve for the death of someone we have never seen—then of the immense and welcome difference which the newly acquired wealth was going to make in their lives.

No more worrying about the essential insecurity of their outwardly comfortable existence. No more dreading the occasional, but violent, outbursts of her father on the subject of any bills other than his own. No more wondering how the family would manage without her when she and Oliver married.

Although to anyone as literal-minded as Alma—or even her father—it might seem that nothing absolutely definite had been arranged between Oliver and herself, to Leslie it had been obvious for some while that, as soon as he had a practice, or the reasonable prospect of one, they would be married. The rest of the family might build their futures round the name of Great-Aunt Tabitha. To Leslie, the future meant Oliver Bendick, whom she had loved for longer than she could remember.

Even in the days when they were schoolchildren, and Oliver was the Doctor's son who knew Morley rather well, while Leslie was merely Morley's sister—even then there had been a degree of understanding and friendship between them which had not existed between any of the other young people of the district. And more than once, after he had got over the inarticulate teens, Oliver had said, "There's no one like you, Leslie. I just couldn't imagine life without you to talk to and plan with."

It was she who had been the recipient of his confidences from the earliest days, she who had sympathized with and encouraged his every ambition. It was to her—even before his parents—he had come with the news that he had passed his final examinations as a doctor. And, now that he was working as a locum less than fifty miles away, she saw him most weekends.

17

She hoped he would be home this weekend, so that she could tell him the news about Great-Aunt Tabitha. To know that the family's future was so clear and satisfactory could not fail to make their own future seem the more secure.

Leslie had several places to visit in the village, and as she entered the little Post Office, which also served as a general haberdashery store, Miss Meeks popped up from behind the counter to enquire personally after the health of the family.

Having reported satisfactorily, Leslie was about to go on to the purchase of stamps when Miss Meeks, leaning towards her in as confidential a manner as her rather rigid corsets would permit, asked, "Did the telegram arrive safely?" as though all sorts of perils might have beset a telegram on its short journey from the Post Office to Cranley Magna.

"The telegram?"

"I sent it up only ten minutes ago, and told Bob to go straight to the house without any loitering." A frown began to gather on Miss Meeks' brow and the faint creaking of her corsets indicated that she was beginning to breathe deeply and with displeasure.

"He probably passed me while I was in Farmers', Miss Meeks. I called in for a paper," Leslie explained, anxious to shield Bob who was Miss Meeks' rather down-trodden nephew.

Miss Meeks suspended judgment for the moment.

"I didn't know you were expecting a visitor," she said casually, as she flicked over her supply of stamps.

"Was the telegram about someone arriving to visit us, then?" Leslie spoke with interest, and never questioned Miss Meeks' inalienable village right to digest and discuss the contents of all telegrams which passed through her hands, either outgoing or incoming.

"I think so. I seem to remember something of the sort." Miss Meeks became falsely reticent all at once.

"Who was it from?" Leslie asked.

"Well, I did notice the name, as it was a strange one. It struck me quite forcibly," Miss Meeks explained, giving the expression almost a physical meaning. "It was signed Reid Carthay. And it said, 'Arriving Thursday.' Which, of course, is today," Miss Meeks pointed out. "That's why I told Bob to hurry."

"Then he'll be coming by the six-twenty, I suppose." Leslie glanced at her watch.

"A friend of the family?" enquired Miss Meeks delicately, as she counted out change.

"A—more sort of a relation," Leslie said. And then thought how much that would have annoyed her father. "I'll have to see about having him met at the station. He won't know that it's a mile and a half from the village, with no chance of a taxi." And she bade Miss Meeks good-bye and went out into the afternoon sunshine once more.

It was still not more than four o'clock, and Leslie reckoned that she had plenty of time to carry out her last commission, which was to collect some honey from a small farm half a mile beyond the village, on the other side from Cranley Magna. And as she walked along the dusty road between the sweet-smelling hedges, she thought about Mr. Reid Carthay and his imminent arrival.

As Morley had said, there was no need to assume that he was an elderly man. But, whatever his age, Leslie hoped he would be sufficiently tolerant in outlook not to mind the various foibles of the Greeves, and not so tender of his dignity that he would resent the slightly hectoring manner which her father would undoubtedly adopt towards one whom he considered to have done him out of the duty and privilege of supervising Great-Aunt Tabitha's funeral.

Leslie collected her honey—two combs of it, dark and of an intoxicating scent—and started homewards. But, before she had gone fifty yards, the sound of a high-powered car coming behind her made her move on to the narrow grass verge at the side of the road.

The car swung round a bend in the lane, passed her at speed, and then drew to an abrupt standstill a little way beyond her. It was a long, low, shining black car of un-English design, and as Leslie came nearer she saw it contained only the driver, a tall, broad-shouldered man, who was obviously waiting for her to come up with him.

Indeed, as she drew abreast of the door, he leaned his arm on the ledge of the open window and said, in a deep voice with a faint accent which she could not quite identify,

"Pardon me. Can you tell me if I'm anywhere near Cranleymere?"

"Yes. That's the village straight ahead." She pointed to the small cluster of houses and two or three village shops which made up Cranleymere.

"*That?*" The man half smiled, with a sort of good-humoured contempt for anything so small. "Is that the whole of it?"

"That's the main part of the village," Leslie said, rather resenting this slight on her home village. "There are a few big houses scattered around as well."

"Including one called Cranley Magna?"

"Why—why, yes." Leslie stared at him, surprised doubt crystallizing into not very pleased certainty. "Are you Mr. Carthay?"

"Sure. I'm Reid Carthay." He smiled completely then, showing strong, even teeth. "Don't tell me you're one of my cousins?"

She had no intention of telling him anything of the sort.

"I'm Leslie Greeve," she said, much more distantly than she usually spoke to anyone. "But we're hardly cousins, are we?"

"Near enough," he assured her easily, and opened the door of the car. "Jump in, Leslie, and I'll drive you up home."

Leslie was not an unfriendly girl, but she felt herself prickle with resentment at this casual familiarity. However, she could hardly refuse a lift from someone who was going to her own home. So she said, "Thank you," coolly, and got into the car.

"Are you the only girl in the family?" he enquired,

as he started the car again, and he spoke as though it were his natural right to ask questions about her.

"No. I have two sisters."

"Both as pretty as you?" He flashed an appreciative smile at her.

Leslie did not take that up. She permitted a slight pause in the conversation, to indicate her opinion of his line of talk, and then added,

"And I have one brother."

"A matter of minor interest," he assured her.

"Not to me. I happen to be fond of my brother. He has nice manners, for one thing," she retorted, surprised to find herself speaking like this.

She was no more surprised than her companion, however. He gave her another quick glance—an amused one—and said,

"What's the sting in that? Think I'm being fresh?"

"I wasn't really thinking about you at all," replied Leslie, with obvious untruth. "Except to wonder, rather apprehensively, about your impact on my father."

"Put that in plain English, would you? Do I turn left here?"

"No. Straight on. And, in plain English, I mean that my father never heard of you until to-day, so that your very existence was something of a sho-surprise. You would do well to remember that and go rather—rather tactfully."

"Implying that I have not exercised tact with you?"

Leslie, who had never before been subjected to the gale of good-humoured candour which seemed to be blowing upon her at the moment, was silent.

Whereat Reid Carthay laughed, put out a hand and, to her inexpressible annoyance, patted her as though she had been a kitten, and said,

"You shouldn't take offence so easily. Is this the drive?"

"Yes." She quickly withdrew her hand from under the strong, warm, brown one which had touched her so easily, and, as they swept round the curve of the

21

drive and came to a stop in front of the house, Alma appeared in the open doorway.

An inquisitive and friendly child by nature, she ran down the steps, and addressed the newcomer with all the curiosity and interest that had been lacking in Leslie.

"Hello! Are *you* Reid Carthay?"

"I am." He leant back, smiling a little, with one hand still resting on the wheel of the car. "Any objections?"

"Oh, no. But I thought you were going to be old."

"There are times when I think I am."

"But I meant *really* old," explained the literal Alma. "You don't look more than forty."

Alma led the way into the drawing-room, where the family was present in force.

Most men, Leslie supposed, would have been slightly intimidated by the spectacle of such a united front, and she would have made the introductions in the friendliest manner possible. But Reid Carthay showed no signs of being put out—much less intimidated—and, having greeted Mrs. Greeve pleasantly and taken in the rest in one comprehensive glance, he shook hands with his host, and said,

"Fortunately, I stopped to ask Leslie the way, so there wasn't much difficulty in finding the place."

Leslie, as they all knew, was the rather reserved one of the family, and to have this man talking as though he and she were old acquaintances made Morley at least glance at her with interest.

"Mr. Carthay," Leslie explained, with the very slightest emphasis on the name, "overtook me just as I left Jenkins' Farm. And, as he asked me the way, of course I guessed who he was."

"Quite, quite," said her father, anxious to monopolize the visitor himself. "Sit down, Carthay, sit down. This is a sad business about poor old Tabitha."

Leslie stole another glance at their visitor.

He didn't *look* a sponger, she reflected. Though of

course that cool air of self-confidence might well be part of his stock-in-trade.

A little more critically, Leslie eyed his admirably tailored dark suit, his unobtrusive but expensive wrist-watch, and recalled the undoubted luxury of the car in which he had given her a lift.

Great-Aunt Tabitha or no, he did remarkably well out of something. Or someone.

He was talking to her mother now, answering the random, conventional questions which one does ask of a stranger who arrives unexpectedly, and seeing him like that, in profile, Leslie was uncomfortably aware of the firmness, even obstinacy, of his jaw and the hard line of his cheek.

He was not just an ordinary sponger, she decided suddenly. Not anything on a small scale. He might be a great rogue or he might be a force for good. But whatever his line, he was big and forceful and probably not a little ruthless. Cranley Magna seemed suddenly rather a delicate, pastel-coloured, unrealistic sort of setting for him, and a vague feeling of apprehension touched Leslie because of it.

However, her mother rose just then to escort their visitor to his room, and the others prepared to scatter, to get ready for tea.

Leslie lingered for a moment to speak to Morley and, seeing this, Katherine came back to join them.

"What did you make of him, Leslie? You seemed to be great friends in a remarkably short time," she said curiously.

"We were nothing of the sort." Leslie spoke with decision. "It was he who made all the advances. I should think he's the kind of man to call you 'honey' the second time he meets you."

"There is a slight American accent," Morley remarked. "I noticed it."

"Oh, that's what it is! I didn't identify it, because there's an overlay of something else."

"Probably a slightly French intonation. He looks the kind of man who's knocked about a good deal."

23

"He settled down pretty close to Great-Aunt Tabitha," remarked Leslie.

But Morley said, "Miaow!" and ruffled her fair hair.

"Why did he *come,* though?" Katherine said reflectively.

"Perhaps he heard that Father had three beautiful daughters, all now richly endowed," suggested Morley. "And he came to look them over."

"Then Kate and Alma can have him between them," Leslie said, with so much energy that her brother and sister both laughed.

She laughed a little herself then, slightly ashamed of her exaggerated resentment of someone who was, after all, a guest, and had not been guilty of anything more than familiarity.

"No, it couldn't have been that," she said, referring back to Morley's flippant suggestion. "I remember now. He asked if I were the only daughter."

"He hoped it all went with you, dear," Morley declared, and laughed again.

"Don't be absurd," Leslie said. Then she remembered that she had left her various purchases in the car, and went out to fetch them.

As she came out of the front door, she saw that he was also there, taking his luggage out of the back of the car, and at the sound of her footsteps he looked up.

He stopped what he was doing immediately, and came to the bottom of the steps and said,

"Look here, I must talk to you. Where can we go?"

Leslie's eyebrows rose slightly and her dark eyes widened with surprise and that queer resentment which she could not control.

"It's almost teatime," she said rather coldly.

"Yes, I know. But there's something I must ask you."

He was so urgent and so authoritative about it that she found herself leading the way to the small shrubbery at the side of the house. But they had hardly moved within the shade of the trees, before she turned to face

24

him and asked, not very promisingly, because she suspected some new, smiling advance,

"Well, what is it?"

He was not smiling, however. He was frowning slightly, and his very keen grey eyes were a little narrowed, as though he were trying to see something a long way off.

"What makes your father think he was old Aunt Tabitha's heir?" was the extraordinary thing he said.

"What makes him think—— Well, because he is, of course. He always has been. She made a will soon after her husband died, when Father was still a schoolboy. We've all known it—all our lives——"

Her rapid assurances trailed off suddenly into silence, and the most horrible, premonitory chill crept down her spine.

"You don't mean—you can't mean—that she *didn't* leave him her money, after all?"

Reid Carthay thrust his hands into his pockets and regarded her almost moodily for a moment, like a man who very much disliked some task he saw in front of him.

"That's exactly what I do mean," he said at last. "She left her money to me. Every damned cent of it. I didn't even know you people existed until I began to look through her correspondence, after she was dead."

CHAPTER TWO

LESLIE had never felt faint in her life, but for a moment it seemed to her that the green and gold and blue of that summer afternoon ran together in one blur, and she clutched at Reid Carthay's arm as though she might fall.

"I'm terribly sorry," he began. Then she recovered herself and stammered,

"No—I'm sorry. I felt—rather strange—for a moment."

"I didn't realize that it would be quite such a shock." He was looking down at her with some concern.

"No. How could you?" She looked round helplessly on a world from which the benevolent security of Great-Aunt Tabitha's influence had departed for ever.

It was difficult, in face of the bright, slightly puzzled glance of this stranger, to explain how completely they had all left everything to chance and Great-Aunt Tabitha. But she felt bound to try.

"We have always—depended on her, you see. On the belief that our futures were secure because we should—should inherit. We built our lives on the expectation—one shouldn't, of course—but we never thought of anything else. We never imagined there could *be* anyone else. We just knew, quite simply, that we were her only real relations."

"Yes. I do see. My people come from the other side, of course. Great-Uncle Leopold's side."

"Oh!" she exclaimed. "Where the money really came from."

"All right. I suppose that is literally true," he agreed. "Though anything there was had belonged to the old lady for nearly half a century."

From the house came the tinkling sound of the tea-bell, and she dragged herself to her feet.

"We shall have to go in. I suppose you—want me to explain things?"

He seemed surprised.

"You? Certainly not. You've had enough shock and nerve-strain already," he said. "I'll tell your father, and he can break the news to the rest as he pleases."

"It will be a fearful shock for him." Her mouth trembled suddenly. "Please be as—gentle as you can about it."

He smiled rather wryly.

"Gentleness isn't much in my line, but I'll do my best."

"Perhaps I'd better do it, after all." Once more she tried to force herself to the task. But he refused to hear of it.

"No, no, you leave that to me. I'll attend to it."

"When?" she asked huskily.

"As soon as tea is over, and I can have a few minutes' private talk with him."

"Very well."

She wondered how she was to get through tea without betraying her agitation, and perhaps he wondered too, because, as they went back into the house, he said,

"You'd better go and fix a bit of colour, hadn't you? They'll notice, if you look as white as that, and think that I've been ill-treating you or something."

She gave a ghost of a laugh.

"Do I look as bad as that?"

He gave her that peculiar, flashing glance of appreciation.

"You look swell," he told her, with the faintest suggestion of a drawl in his voice. "But you need the illusion of a little red blood in your cheeks."

She said nothing to that, and went away upstairs to her room, leaving him to find his own way back to the drawing-room.

In her bedroom she stood before the mirror and stared at her white reflection, while she tried to take in what had really happened. As the realization of the disaster stabbed her afresh, one or two sobbing gasps of sheer fright and distress escaped her.

Then she pulled herself together and told herself

not to be a coward. And after touching her cheeks with colour and adding a little lipstick to her mouth, she deliberately assumed an air of casual unconcern.

"There's always Oliver," she told herself, leaning on that final security with infinite relief. "I'll think of something for the family. Poor darlings, it's going to be fearful for them. But at least I have Oliver. What should I do, if I hadn't him?"

As soon as tea was over, their visitor got up and said to his host,

"May I have a word or two with you, sir, in private? It's a matter of business."

"Of course, of course." Richard Greeve, who had never done a stroke of business in his life, always assumed an air of importance and understanding when the word was mentioned. And he led the way to his study rather, Leslie thought with pity, like a very large and inoffensive lamb leading the way, unknowingly, to the slaughter.

The door closed behind the two men, and Alma said, in a tone of enjoyment,

"I bet he's going to talk to Father about the will, and tell him how much money there is."

Leslie bit her lip at the grimly unconscious truth of that. But her mother said placidly,

"He wouldn't know about that, dear."

"Mother, what makes you think so?" Leslie's voice was a little breathless, but she felt impelled to say something, anything, which might in some small way prepare them for the shock that was coming.

"Why, as your father said, he isn't really *in* the family, Leslie. He wouldn't know anything important. He seems an agreeable sort of man, though inclined to throw his weight about a little. He wouldn't be likely to know anything about Great-Aunt Tabitha's really private affairs. Your father said not."

Leslie wanted to say that Father didn't know everything—that it was useless to quote him, in face of the advancing tide. But she restrained herself, and only said quite quietly,

28

"I think we must accept the fact that Mr. Carthay knew Great-Aunt Tabitha a great deal better than we did. He actually lived in the same place, remember, for something like a year. She—may have grown very fond of him, and felt he was the—the only member of her family she had near her."

"And he is rather nice, anyway," Alma remarked judicially.

"Old ladies would adore him, I'm sure." Morley rubbed his chin meditatively. "Masterful is, I believe, the word which would describe him in their vocabulary."

"And suppose she did adore him——" Leslie looked straight across at her brother, her eyes wide in her pale face. "What would she be most likely to do?"

"I wouldn't know the answer to that," her brother replied regretfully, "never having been an old lady's darling."

But Alma, with the awful simplicity of the completely literal-minded, said,

"She might leave him her money, I suppose."

"Exactly," Lelie agreed. And silence fell like a stone among them.

"What—do you mean?" Slowly Katherine turned and stared wide-eyed in her turn. "Why do you say 'exactly' in that Greek tragedy tone? You don't mean that you think *Great-Aunt Tabitha* might have left *him* her money?"

"I mean that I know she did," Leslie said, and expelled her long-held breath in a sigh which almost hurt.

"What?" they all chorused, except for Mrs. Greeve.

"What Leslie says is perfectly true," Reid Carthay's voice said dryly from the doorway and turning, with one accord, they found him standing there, surveying the scene with bright, hard eyes and a rather grim expression.

He came slowly forward into the room then, seeming to dominate the situation without any apparent effort.

29

"I'm sorry——" He looked round on them all, but even when his glance rested on Mrs. Greeve, it did not appreciably soften. "I understand that this must be a great shock for you all. But let us have it quite clear from the beginning—there has been no dirty work on my part. You are perhaps a little more closely related to the old lady than I am. I am perhaps a little more closely related to the money than you are." A faint, sardonic smile just touched his lips. "When all is said and done, however, she was entitled to leave her money exactly as she pleased. I never discussed it with her. For all I knew, she had left the lot to a home for canaries——"

"Was there an awful lot of money?" interrupted Alma, who could not suppress a sort of gloomy curiosity about it, even though it had ceased to concern them personally.

"Not so much as your father seemed to expect."

"Oh, poor Richard!" His wife sprang to her feet. "This will be worse for him than any of us. I must go to him."

With a glance of unmerited reproach at their guest, she brushed past him and out of the room. As she did so, the telephone bell rang shrilly in the hall.

Leslie supposed it was cowardly of her to seize this chance of escape from a scene which was becoming unbearably tense. But, before anyone else could move to do so, she went to answer the telephone. And, as she lifted the receiver and put it to her ear, to her immeasurable relief it was Oliver's voice which said,

"Hello. Is that you, Leslie?"

"Oh, *yes*, Oliver!" She didn't attempt to keep the relief and delight out of her voice. "I wasn't expecting you home yet. I'm so glad you're here. There's some—some news, and I want to—tell you about it."

"Well, that's a coincidence." Oliver was smiling, she could tell from his tone. "I have some news too, and I want to tell you about it."

"My news isn't very nice."

But, even as she uttered this piece of under-statement,

she felt her spirits rise. No news could be quite so terrible if Oliver were home and in such obviously good spirits.

"I *am* sorry. What's happened? May I come over?"

She started to say, "Yes, of course," and then she changed her mind, for there was going to be little chance of a private chat with Oliver, or anyone else, in the house that evening.

"I'll walk over to meet you," she said quickly. "Come by way of the woods, and I'll meet you at the crossroads."

"The old spot?" He laughed and added, "That's rather appropriate somehow," before he rang off. For the "crossroads" in the woods—an open space where two paths met—had been a favourite meeting-place of the young Greeves and Oliver Bendick when they were schoolchildren, and a good many confidences had been exchanged there over the years.

Leslie replaced the receiver and cast a glance towards the closed drawing-room door, from behind which came a murmur of voices. There were the characteristic, full overtones of the family, mingling in such a way that it was difficult to distinguish one from another. And then, almost symbolically, there cut across the hum that cool, incisive, alien tone, carrying with it the suggestion of authority which she had noticed before.

Leslie could not distinguish any actual words, but whatever Reid Carthay had said reduced the others to silence. And, fearing for some new development which might interfere with her meeting Oliver, she hastily slipped out of the house, having paused only long enough to leave word with Jessie, their elderly and devoted maid, that she had gone across to the Bendicks' place and might not be in to supper.

Although she had walked rapidly, Leslie saw, as soon as she came in sight of their meeting-place, that Oliver was before her. He was sitting on a fallen tree-trunk, which had been there and made a rough seat for them all almost since she could remember. But, at the sight of her, he sprang to his feet and came towards her.

In that moment he epitomized for Leslie all which was still secure and familiar and worthwhile. Dark and rather slight, but with an intelligent head and the strong, beautiful hands of a born surgeon, Oliver Bendick had that indefinable something which we call personality. And, as he took both her hands in his light, firm clasp Leslie gave a quick sigh of relief and felt the last of her dark apprehensions slide from her.

Indeed, when Oliver said, "Come and tell me what the trouble is," it seemed absurd to spoil the radiance of the evening and the joy of their meeting by going over the melancholy story again. Her instinct was to thrust all recollection of Great-Aunt Tabitha and Reid Carthay from her, and she exclaimed,

"No. Tell me your news first. I think I've been exaggerating the gloom of mine. Let's talk of something nice."

"Sure?" He looked at her, amused and questioning, but with an air of suppressed excitement too, which told her how eager he was to talk of his own affairs.

"Quite sure. Let's sit down." And they retraced their steps to the fallen tree-trunk and sat down side by side—he still holding one of her hands, she noticed.

"It's all happened so suddenly, Leslie, I can hardly believe in it even now." His dark, lively face was lit up by enthusiasm and pleasure. "You remember the Frentons——"

She searched her memory and recalled the family of an elderly doctor, with whom Oliver had made friends during his time as a locum.

"Yes." She nodded.

"Well, I was there last weekend, and I had a long talk with old Dr. Frenton. We've had many talks, of course—more than I realized—and he'd drawn me out a good deal on my various theories and intentions. Again more than I had realized. And then he told me, Leslie, that he'd been turning over in his mind for some time the idea of taking me into partnership, and he'd finally decided to do so."

"You mean—just like that?" She was as astonished

and delighted as any news-bringer could wish.

"Well," he laughed, "there are some conditions and arrangements to discuss, naturally. But it is virtually settled, and I feel I can already look forward to building the exact type of future that my heart was really set on. You see, it's a big and varied practice. So many opportunities for following up the ideas I've been working on for years. Such a chance——"

He broke off and, smiling thoughtfully, looked away from her through the trees, as though already he saw vistas of absorbing work and heart-warming achievement. Until now the choice for him had lain simply between a regulation government appointment or the taking over of his father's diminishing country practice in a sparsely populated neighbourhood where another youngish doctor was already the really important figure.

"It would mean living in town, of course—in Pencaster," Leslie said quietly and thoughtfully, because she did not want to disturb his happy reflections. At the same time, she was longing to hear more of something which, she felt, must so closely affect herself.

His eyes—and his attention—came back to her.

"Yes, in Pencaster. And that brings me to the second part of my news."

"Oh, there is some more?" Her lips parted in eager interest, and he laughed aloud.

"Leslie, you're marvellous!" he declared. "The best audience anyone ever had."

She laughed too then, pleased and indefinably excited, because she sensed considerable excitement in him.

"You're just like a sister listening to a favourite brother's airy-fairy plans." Oliver looked at her affectionately. "Except, I suppose," he added reflectively, "that most brothers don't appreciate sisterly interest as much as I appreciate yours. Maybe that's because I have no sisters."

She smiled—but a little doubtfully that time, for the brother-sister relationship was not one that she herself had ever thought of in connection with Oliver and herself. It was true, of course, that he had been like one of the family for so long that the expression did describe their degree of intimacy. But she wished he had used some other term, and she said rather quickly,

"Well, go on. Tell me the rest."

"I haven't told anyone else yet except Mother," he said earnestly. "But I'd like you to be the first to know, outside my own family, Leslie. I'm going to be married. And one of the nicest things about it all is that Caroline is old Dr. Frenton's niece—it was through her that I met him—so everything has worked in together in the most wonderful way."

Leslie thought there was an odd little silence, then, to her surprise, she heard someone say, "Why, how splendid!" And, to her further surprise, she realized that it was herself.

She didn't really think at all in the next few moments. Not with the surface of her mind, that was to say. Only, deep down in her subconscious, some instinct prompted her to say, "Tell me some more about it. What is she like?" Because those words would force him to further speech, and so put some sort of shield between any perception of his and her own naked, appalled dismay.

His voice went on and, to the best of her belief, she smiled and looked attentive. But nothing which he said really reached her. It was as though some small, vital connection were broken, and she sat there, isolated from the rest of the world by the immensity of what had just happened. Only some obstinate core of pride— some instinct of self-preservation—helped her to play her role so that Oliver should never, never guess what a fool she had been, or what a blow he had dealt her.

But she dragged her mind back from such reflections as that. Unless she kept every scrap of her remaining attention on what Oliver was saying, she would betray herself. And so, while part of her seemed to stand aside in stunned and leaden detachment, the rest of her played —perhaps slightly over-played—the role of the interested, sisterly confidante.

He was not, however—as she guessed—in a mood to

be critical of a good audience. He wanted to talk of his happiness, and if she would listen and smile and put in a word here and there, that was all he needed. Indeed, it was not until she rose finally, and said that she must be going home, that he recollected affairs other than his own, and exclaimed,

"Good lord! I've done all the talking, I'm afraid. What was it that you were going to tell me, Leslie?"

"Tell you?" She looked vague for a moment, for she could not imagine there was anything she could have to tell the stranger that Oliver had become.

"Yes. You said you'd had some bad news at home or something."

"Oh—Great-Aunt Tabitha died."

She made the statement almost indifferently, for Great-Aunt Tabitha and her place in the scheme of things had shrunk all at once to inconsiderable proportions.

But Oliver was impressed. Living so close to the Greeves, and being so much one of them, he naturally knew all the implications which this announcement carried with it.

"It's not exactly bad news, surely? I mean—the old lady was a stranger really. And even the most tender-hearted and disinterested person never minded inheriting a fortune."

"We haven't inherited a fortune, after all."

"What!"

"There's a—a nephew or cousin or something." Oh, she couldn't go over it all again, she felt. Not now. With every feeling raw and protesting. So she compromised, hastily if a little untruthfully, by saying, "We don't know the exact position yet. But we think it's—it's going to be rather disappointing financially."

"Leslie, I am sorry!" He looked grave, and obviously made a valiant attempt to subdue his own radiant spirits to a level more in keeping with the misfortune of his friends.

"Oh, it may not be so bad as we feared at first." She smiled with determined cheerfulness, because she longed now to escape, and her uppermost thought was that this conversation must not be allowed to take a new lease of life.

"How did your father take the news?"

"I'm not quite sure."

"You're not sure?" He looked astonished.

"I mean that I—came away to meet you without having seen him after the news had been broken to him."

"I say, it was pretty good of you to come here and listen to my vapourings with all that anxiety on your mind," he exclaimed sincerely.

"Oh, no. I thought——" She broke off and smiled vaguely, because that was the only expression with which she could hide the fact that her mouth was suddenly trembling. "I felt sure that whatever you had to say would cheer me, and"—a supreme effort, but she made it—"it certainly has. I'm so—glad for you, Oliver. But—I must go now to the family," she repeated.

"Yes, of course." He took her hand and wrung it. "Is there anything I could do? Would it be any help if I came along?"

"No, I don't think so." She managed to say that consideringly, instead of on a note of hysterical protest. "I'll—let you know how things are."

"Very well." He repeated his assurances of good will and, as far as she could remember afterwards, she somehow repeated her congratulations. And then, at last, she was free to go—hurrying from him as though her remembered family responsibilities were what drove her on, and not just the terrible, devouring wish to flee from the scene where she had suffered such unutterable humiliation and shock.

Presently, when she knew she was completely out of his sight, she slackened her pace and, with a gesture of weariness and defeat, put up her hand to push back the heavy fair hair from her forehead.

But her hand never reached her hair. Instead, she suddenly found that she was desperately wiping the tears from her face—while she sobbed aloud, and dropped to the ground.

"I ought to have seen what had happened," she told herself fiercely. "I should have, but for our fatal family failing of ignoring realities and just waiting complacently for life to deliver the goods we most want. I'll never, never, never be caught like this again! I'll never believe *anything* I want to believe until it's been proved to the hilt."

The very intensity of her painful resolution forced another sob or two from her. And then to her horrified ears came a sound which drove her to the final depths of humiliation. Someone was coming towards her—she could hear the light crackle of twigs underfoot as he came—and she knew it was a contrite Oliver, coming to reinforce what he doubtless felt had been rather perfunctory expressions of sympathy.

What would he think, finding her here in a passion of tears? What was she to say, caught thus at a complete disadvantage, and stripped of every shred of dignity or defensive pride?

Although she knew he had dropped down on the grass beside her, she resolutely kept her face hidden, as though by doing so she might put off the terrible moment when he must speak, and show in his embarrassed and horrified tone that he had guessed the truth.

To her despairing fancy, the silent moments measured themselves out to incalculable length, punctuated only by a couple of stifled after-sobs from her which betrayed the passion of her previous outburst.

And then he spoke at last, and it was not Oliver's voice. It was Reid Carthay, who said on a note of not unkindly protest.

"Oh, come, honey, don't cry like that. No lost fortune was ever worth so many tears." And she was scooped up, a little unceremoniously but with some dexterity, and found herself leaning exhaustedly against the family intruder, who was regarding her with a sort of humorous dismay.

CHAPTER THREE

LESLIE'S first impulse was to exclaim that no mere lost fortune would have made her cry so tempestuously. But the next moment she realized that, all unknowing, he had offered her a straw at which her drowning pride might clutch. Neither he nor anyone else need ever know the tragic folly which had prompted these tears.

Mildly embarrassing it might be to be thought capable of weeping unrestrainedly over the loss of a hoped-for fortune. But that was nothing to the agony of humiliation involved in anyone guessing the real truth.

So, instead of pulling away from him with some indignant denial, she continued to lean against his arm for a moment—not altogether averse to having this support in her limp and exhausted condition—and said,

"I don't—usually cry—about such things. But it's a little—frightening to realize how different the future is going to be from anything we ever expected."

"Yes, I can understand that."

"Kate and I can manage well enough, I don't doubt. And I suppose Alma will just go on being at school. Though it may have to be a very different school, of course," she murmured in parenthesis. "But—Morley. And Mother and Father——"

"Um-hm," he agreed, rubbing his chin reflectively. "I've gathered that your parents constitute a formidable part of the problem."

"It's easy enough to criticize them," she exclaimed quickly and defensively—and now she did pull away from him, sitting up and trying, with a hasty hand, to smooth her tumbled hair. "It's true that they've lived a comfortable, unrealistic sort of life based on little more than fond hopes. You can say they're silly and out-dated and all that sort of thing, but——"

"I wasn't really going to say anything of the kind, you know," he put in mildly.

"But the fact is that they've made a lovely home-life for us here—always," she ran on, not heeding his interruption. "Except for what happened to Morley, we've been a completely happy family. I don't think anyone can ever have been happier or more—more carefree." As she looked back on past contentment, unlikely ever to return, her voice trembled for a moment, and in her effort to steady it once more she achieved a hard, almost resentful tone. "You can't say they've done nothing worthwhile, when they've made their four children happy all these years."

"No one is suggesting they've done nothing worthwhile—least of all myself, my sweet," he returned, and that drawl which tended to broaden his vowels at times was very marked. "I'm not here to comment on the past. I'm here to see what can be done about the future."

"Do you mean—*our* future?" she asked incredulously.

"Your future," he confirmed easily.

"But we aren't—exactly—your business, are we?"

"No?" He smiled at her, so compellingly that she blushed a little and looked away. "You're my only relations—so far as I know."

"We aren't relations!" Her father's remembered insistence on that point gave added emphasis to her denial. "At least, it's a relationship of the very remotest kind."

"The best type possible," he assured her, and that lazy smile seemed to travel over her again in a way no man had dared to smile at her before. "Just enough to constitute a claim to notice, and not enough to lapse into conventional dullness."

"I don't know what you mean," she said quickly. But, suddenly, for no special reason, she had a clear recollection of Oliver saying she was like a sister to him, and she thought that in no circumstances whatever would Reid Carthay choose to regard her as a sister.

"I'll explain in more detail, if you like," he offered amusedly.

But she said hastily, "No, thank you." And when he laughed, she added, "I don't see what you think you could do about our future."

"No?" He punched little holes in the turf with his thumb and smiled to himself. "The situation isn't all that obscure, you know. You folk have always expected to have the money that has suddenly come to me. It seems you even had very good reason to feel that way. That being so, I can't do less than see you get some of it, surely."

"Nonsense!" She was startled, and a little indignant again. "Father wouldn't hear of such a thing."

Reid Carthay looked sceptical.

"He's in a rather nasty spot if he won't."

"I'm sure he is. But that wouldn't make him take money from a—a stranger. He's quite proud in his own way, you know."

"I'm glad you had the grace to hesitate before handing me the word 'stranger.' " He glanced up at her with a grin. "But, apart from that, your father has quite a strong moral right to some of this money, by any standards."

"He wouldn't think so," Leslie insisted. And she hoped rather agitatedly that she was right, for it made her feel oddly uncomfortable to think of their being under a great obligation to this bold, smiling man.

"Then will you tell me what he—indeed all of you— can do as an alternative?"

The question was not offensively put, but it had a sort of good-humoured, irresistible logic about it. And she was silent, because, of course, there was no easy answer to that.

"It's too early to say," she declared at last. "We haven't had time to do more than—than take in the essential fact."

"Well, at least promise me not to cry about it any more," he said, getting up and holding out his hand to her.

She longed to tell him, even then, that she had not been crying about that, for she hated to be thought so spineless. But the alternative of even hinting at the truth was so unthinkable that she could only put her hand into his and allow him to help her to her feet, while she said,

"I shan't cry any more." And in her heart she added rather bitterly, "Not even about Oliver." For he belonged to someone else now—to Caroline Frenton. And to cry about some other girl's man was the final humiliation.

When they reached home, she could hardly believe that it was only just supper-time. It seemed to her that she had lived through almost a lifetime of experience since she had left the house. And now here was Alma hopping up and down on one foot and chanting, "Cold chicken for supper," just as though the world had not been turned upside down.

Somewhat to the embarrassment of the younger Greeves, neither of their parents appeared at supper-time, and they were left to entertain the stranger as best they could.

And then at last supper was over, and when Katherine suggested they should have coffee in the drawing-room, to the profound relief of everyone Reid replied that he didn't want any coffee, but would take his car and drive around and have a look at the district.

After he had gone, they all remained silent for a few minutes. Then Alma said rather defiantly,

"I like him."

"*Do* you?" Katherine flicked her gold-tipped lashes effectively. "I can't help feeling what a relief it is to have our home to ourselves again!"

"But I think he means well," Leslie said.

"A confoundedly dull tribute to pay anyone," declared Morley. "I hope he isn't going to thrust his money down our throats. I've always had a sneaking sympathy with the *nouveaux riches* before. But really they mustn't be quite so *nouveaux* or quite so *riches*."

41

And, for a moment, he looked extraordinarily like his father.

"Oh—I don't know." Suddenly Leslie felt a most rare irritation with her family, and more particularly with Morley. And because the last thing she wanted was to make Reid a bone of contention in the family circle, she got up and said, "I think I'll take a tray up to Mother and see how she's feeling. I do wish she wouldn't behave as though there'd been a death in the house, poor pet."

The others laughed. But with an air of surprise and indulgence. For they were still judging the situation from the family standard of values, while she, Leslie realized with surprise, was beginning to wonder how these things would appear to an outsider.

Puzzled and faintly disturbed by the discovery, she arranged a tempting little meal on a tray, and went upstairs.

"Come in, darling," her mother's voice said plaintively, when she knocked at the door of the pretty, pastel-tinted, Greuze-like room which presented such a perfect setting for its owner. And, as Leslie entered, her mother turned a faintly tear-marked face towards her, and languidly shifted one or two of the frilled pillows of the sofa on which she was reclining.

"How do you feel, dear?" Leslie's voice instinctively softened and took on an indulgent note.

"I'm all right, Leslie. It's your poor father I am thinking about. And Morley." Tears came again into the beautiful dark eyes.

"Yes, I know. It's been a bad shock for us all. But I have a feeling things aren't going to be as bad as we feared," Leslie insisted cheerfully, as she propped up her mother against the cushions and gave her the tray.

"I don't really want anything to eat," Mrs. Greeve said sadly. But she looked with interest at what her daughter had set out, and presently she began to do reasonable justice to the meal, while Leslie sat on a low seat near the sofa and made encouraging comments from time to time.

"I'm glad you feel so hopeful and cheerful about things, darling," she said, looking with an air of melancholy indulgence at her daughter. "But then, of course," she added with a sigh, "all this won't affect you so deeply as the rest of us."

"Oh, Mother! Do you think I don't share the family anxieties?"

"Of course, my dear. But you have other plans to make you happy. You haven't actually said anything about it, I know. But you and Oliver——"

"Oh, no!" Leslie cried sharply, and her mother stopped and looked at her in surprise.

Leslie bit her lip and tried to smile quite casually. Deep down in her heart was a sort of relief that she had not been the only one to read the situation wrongly. If her mother too had thought Oliver loved her, then perhaps she had not been so foolish and self-deluding to allow herself that belief. But she could not allow her mother, or anyone else, to continue in that fond error. And so, after a moment, she managed to say lightly,

"Don't make any romances between Oliver and any of your daughters, darling. He's just got engaged to some girl in Pencaster and her uncle is going to take him into partnership—and everything in his particular garden is just fine."

"But, my *dear*——" Leslie wished her mother would not look quite so dismayed and astonished. It recalled for an agonizing moment what she herself had felt when Oliver first told her of Caroline Frenton. "I felt certain —I thought you did too——" Mrs. Greeve stopped again, and suddenly her whole manner changed. Her vague and elegant melancholy was gone, and for a moment she became any mother anxious over her hurt child.

"Was it a great shock to you, darling?" she asked, so simply and tenderly that Leslie put her head down against her mother's arm for a long minute and was silent.

"One gets over these things," she said at last, without

looking up. "You mustn't think my heart's broken or anything like that." Somehow she must minimize things if she were to save her mother further anxiety. "But— I was very fond of him, of course. More like a sister perhaps." She even forced herself to say the hated word. "But I was rather shaken when he told me."

"When did he tell you?"

"This evening."

"Oh, dear——" Mrs. Greeve stroked the bright head against her arm. "Everything seems to be happening at once."

"Maybe it's better that way, so that they can cancel each other out," Leslie suggested, with an unsteady laugh.

"I wish there were something to help cancel out the shock your father has had," Mrs. Greeve said with a sigh.

"Oh—I meant to tell you. Reid had a talk with me. He has an idea that Father ought to have at least some of Great-Aunt Tabitha's money. He says he has a moral right to it."

Her mother made no scornful protests about that, as Morley and even Leslie herself had done. She thoughtfully considered what her daughter had reported.

"He is right, of course," she said finally. "But I doubt if your father will see things that way. His pride has been terribly hurt over being omitted from the will, quite apart from the financial disaster involved. I don't think he'd agree to take money from a stranger, even in the present dreadful situation."

"Reid isn't exactly a stranger," Leslie found herself saying.

Her mother regarded her consideringly, as though she were mentally measuring her husband's obstinacy against that of the newcomer. But when she spoke what she said was,

"I wish he'd fall in love with Kate."

"Mother, what an extraordinary thing to say!"

"And she with him, of course. Then he could marry her, and it would keep all the money in the family

44

without hurting your father's pride. Or Morley's," she added as an afterthought. "Morley is going to be very difficult too."

"Yes, I know. He's shown signs of it already."

"Well—it's hard for him," Morley's mother said with a sigh. And they were both silent, thinking what it must be like to be the one young man in the family— and virtually helpless in this crisis.

"Has your father had any supper?" Mrs. Greeve asked at last.

"No, I don't think so."

"Then I'd better go and see what I can do with him." And in one graceful movement Mrs. Greeve rose from the sofa.

And Leslie, picking up the tray and preparing to follow her, wondered if, after all, their mother were quite such a sweet and helpless creature as they all supposed. Or was it that those very soft and feminine women had hidden strength and understanding where their own were concerned?

Leslie returned the tray to the kitchen, noticed that it was past Alma's bedtime, and routed out her younger sister and despatched her, protesting, to bed. Then she went to her own room where, for half an hour at least, she could be alone with her thoughts and take mental stock of all that had happened on this most momentous day of her life.

Someone knocked on the door just then, and she called, "Come in" and then sat up and opened her eyes as Katherine came in.

"Hello." Katherine dropped down gracefully on the end of Leslie's bed. "I just thought I'd like a sisterly exchange of ideas. At the moment, I find it difficult to realize that I'm still myself."

Leslie smiled.

"I'd just come round to thinking the same thing, and trying to decide what the future looked like. By the way"—and she admired the casualness of her own voice as she spoke—"I forgot to tell you all, with so much more going on in the family circle, Oliver has just become engaged."

"Oliver!" Katherine sat up and gave her sister an odd glance. "To whom?"

"A girl in Pencaster of whom I've never heard. She's called Caroline Frenton, and her uncle's taking Oliver into partnership."

"How—extraordinary. I always rather thought he might marry you."

"Did you? So did I—when I was about seventeen," Leslie said, and laughed quite naturally.

"Oh, it was like that, was it?" Katherine dismissed the affair carelessly. "I'm glad it went no deeper." Then she rolled over on her back on the bed and stared at the ceiling. "Now the family fortunes have failed, I suppose you and I are going to have to think seriously about finding rich husbands."

"Or good jobs."

"I'm not the stuff of which career-women are made, myself," Katherine said, and laughed. "I shall concentrate on the rich husband."

Leslie was silent. And in the silence they both heard a car coming up the drive.

"There's one rich possibility approaching the house at the moment," Leslie remarked dryly, thinking of what her mother had said.

"I know. But I don't think I could fall in love with him."

"You're asking rather a lot, aren't you?" Leslie said with a smile. "A rich husband *and* a love match."

When Katherine finally rose to go, and declared that she was suddenly very sleepy, Leslie got up too and said,

"I think I'll run downstairs for ten minutes. If Mother and Father haven't been talking to Reid, he'll think it queer and unfriendly that no one bothers even to say good night to him."

"All right. You go and look after his wounded feelings," Katherine replied with a laugh, and she departed to her own room.

Leslie went rather slowly downstairs. The house was very quiet now, but there was a light still on in the drawing-room and the door stood half open. For a moment she thought the room was empty. But when she came in, she saw that he was standing by one of the big windows, looking out into the darkened garden.

He could not have noticed her footsteps, or else he was very deep in thought, because she was half-way across the room before he turned rather sharply to face her.

"I'm sorry. Did I startle you? I'm afraid my steps didn't sound much on this carpet."

"No. I saw your reflection in the window-pane."

She came over to stand beside him, and looked out into the night.

"Did you have a nice drive?"

"Very, thank you."

She felt, rather than saw, that he was looking down at her with amused attention and, though she would not glance up at him, her social conscience stirred a little within her, so that she said,

"I hope you haven't been all on your own since you came in."

"No. I had a talk with your parents."

"Oh?" She did glance up then. "With any—result?"

He smiled wryly.

"I discovered you were right when you said your father had his pride—if you call that getting results."

"You mean he wouldn't listen to your proposition about—about the money?"

"No. But I hardly expected him to at first. I suppose I can consider that I won a minor victory, however, in that he pressed me to stay on here some while. As he gets to know me better, he may change his mind a little."

"And you're prepared to stay on here, just in the hope that he will presently agree to accept some of your money? You're an extraordinary man," she said slowly.

"That isn't my only reason for wishing to stay."

47

"No? I'm afraid you'll find it rather dull here. We're nearly twenty miles from a town of any size."

"I know. Pencaster, isn't it?"

"Yes." She glanced enquiringly at him. "Did you go there this evening?"

"No. But I knew it was near here when I came."

"How odd you should have heard of it. It isn't of any special importance, you know. Just a rather nice market town, with a slightly smarter population than that usually implies."

"Is that so?"

"How did you hear of it?"

He hesitated a moment. Then he said,

"I was engaged to a girl who came from there."

"You were—— *Were* you?" Somehow it surprised her profoundly that he should have been engaged, or that, having been so, he had not piloted (or driven) the affair to a successful conclusion. "Is that the other reason why you are interested in staying on here?" she enquired, before she could stop herself.

He smiled, but again he hesitated.

"It could be. I have a certain—natural curiosity about her, let us say."

"Was it all a good while ago?"

"About a year."

Something hard in his voice told her that he was recalling a period which had meant a great deal to him, and which even now could not be resigned without pain. With her own unfortunate experience so fresh in her mind, she felt a little throb of sympathy for him, and perhaps that sounded in her voice as she said,

"Did she—leave you?"

He nodded.

"I'm sorry. It—hurt a lot, didn't it?"

"Like hell," he said, but he grinned at her ruefully.

Leslie sighed.

"I know. It does."

"Do you mean that you really know?" he enquired. "Or was that just a general comment?"

She withdrew quickly into her shell again.

"Oh, I wasn't thinking of any personal experience, if that's what you mean."

"That's what I meant," he agreed.

She was anxious to shift the talk from her own affairs, and so she asked with more curiosity than she might otherwise have displayed,

"Are you hoping to—win her back?"

"My dear, I'm taking this admirable opportunity of—exploring the position, that's all."

"I see." She looked out of the darkened window again, and then back at him. "If it's any help to—bring her here, or—use us as a background——"

He interrupted with a slight laugh which sounded friendly.

"That's sweet of you. A family background might certainly give me a little more stability in Caroline's eyes, I suppose. She disapproved of my independent, lone-wolf existence."

Leslie swallowed slightly, and a faint, superstitious chill touched her.

"Did you say her name was—Caroline?"

He frowned.

"Did I mention her name? I didn't mean to. But it is Caroline."

"Not—Caroline Frenton, by any chance?"

For a long moment he stared at her, his eyes slightly narrowed, as though he suspected some sort of trap. Then he said,

"How did you know?"

"I didn't. It just—seemed inevitable," Leslie murmured under her breath.

"I don't understand." His voice was cold, and no longer friendly. "Do you know Caroline?"

"No. Only of her. She became engaged today to—to someone I know very well."

"I see," he said. And then, almost casually, "Was that why you were crying so bitterly when I found you this evening?"

CHAPTER FOUR

FOR a few moments Leslie said nothing—stunned by the terrible accuracy with which Reid had guessed her feelings for Oliver.

"No one knows," she gasped at last, catching her breath in her anxiety. "Except Mother. And even she doesn't know quite how—how important he was to me."

"All right. I shan't tell anyone, if that's what you mean."

He looked rather moodily away from her into the darkness.

"So Caroline is engaged," he said slowly, as though he were forcing the words into his own consciousness. And then she realized that what she had said must have been a blow for him.

"I'm dreadfully sorry! I was so surprised that I didn't think what I was saying—didn't prepare you for what I was going to say. I'm afraid it was a shock."

"Well, I guess what I said was something of a shock for you too," he returned, with a slight grimace.

"Not so much as what Oliver said," she murmured. And then she was surprised and dismayed afresh to find that she seemed unable to keep herself from saying just what came into her mind. "Please forget that," she added urgently.

"Honey," he said, and he put his arm round her with an unsentimental good-humour impossible to resent,"you and I know a little too much about each other now for either of us to risk telling tales. I'll forget whatever you please about your Oliver if you'll undertake not to remember too much of what I've said about Caroline."

"One doesn't actually forget these things, of course," she said with a sigh. "But I promise not to speak about them, and you've already done the same."

"Fine." He smiled down at her. "Are you feeling a little better for having someone else in the same boat?"

"Oh! That wouldn't be either kind or logical," Leslie declared, avoiding a direct answer, because she was a trifle ashamed to realize that her heart had felt curiously lighter ever since he had told her that he had once been engaged to Caroline Frenton.

"What is he like, Leslie?"

"Oliver?" She looked up, startled. "Why, he's—dark and good-looking and—clever."

"The kind most girls would fall for, in fact."

She smiled faintly, but with a sort of obstinate courage.

"I can only say that I fell for him. But then I'd known him most of my life."

"Poor kid! I hadn't realized that."

She frowned, because she didn't think that, even in this new mood of shared confidences, she could bear the pity of a stranger, when her own mother's compassion had hurt.

"Why did you ask about him?" she said curiously.

"I was wondering whether the whole thing could be a temporary infatuation. Something I could get Caroline over."

"Do you mean—*try to take her away* from Oliver?"

She was shocked and showed it. But he laughed without contrition.

"She was mine first," he reminded her.

"But that's over now."

He looked at her humorously and said, "Here, whose side are you on?"

"Neither! At least—I mean——"

And then she was silent, because she was realizing, with the clearness given to a scene revealed by a flash of lightning, just what it would mean to her if Reid carried out his threat, and carried it out successfully.

"But Caroline is happily engaged to Oliver now," she protested, with a tenth of the conviction she had shown before.

"How do you know she is?"

"He told me so! It's his happiness too," she cried,

51

with remorseful fervour, remembering how bemused and enraptured Oliver had looked as he talked of his engagement. "You mustn't interfere now, Reid, between two people who love each other."

"Or think they do," he retorted. "Suppose I tell you that she loved me and that I still love her." He smiled, but in a curiously obstinate way that tightened the line of his jaw and made his eyes seem light and brilliant.

"I'm sure she did once and that you still love her. Just as I—I love Oliver," she said with an effort. "But we're outside the present framework, Reid. We're just the—unlucky ones. We must accept the fact—resign ourselves to——"

"My sweet, I never resigned myself to anything in my life," he broke in dryly. "I am not resigned to the present situation."

"But you can't *do* things like that. There are some decencies that one observes!"

"Good lord! he isn't married to her yet," Reid retorted carelessly. "I'm not setting out to snaffle another man's wife."

"But they are engaged. It's the first step towards their marriage."

"People can retrace first steps."

"Reid, I can't understand your talking like this. I haven't known you long, it's true, but I could have sworn you were not this sort of man."

"What sort?" he wanted to know with genuinely amused curiosity.

"Why, the sort who would try to upset someone else's love story, of course. You've *lost*. Can't you be a better loser than this?"

He frowned thoughtfully and, since she had moved from him a little in her indignation and earnestness, he took his arm away from her.

"Look, Leslie," he said at last, and his tone was as earnest now as hers. "The circumstances of our parting weren't exactly simple, or above-board. I found out recently that someone told her lies about me—it doesn't matter now who or why. It was because she thought something quite wrong about me that she manufactured a quarrel and broke the engagement. As soon as I heard the real story, I came after her—it coincided very well with my coming to see your people too, incidentally—to find if I could mend things. And, in the circumstances, I'm damned if I'm going to stand aside for a day-old engagement to someone else. Someone you might well comfort if he lost out, I might add."

"No! Don't add that! Leave me out of your calculations," Leslie cried agitatedly, because the leap of her heart frightened her. "Oh, I—don't know what to say. If what you say it true, it—it's terribly hard on you, of course. But then there is Oliver and *his* happiness."

"Which is genuinely the most important thing to you in all this?" he said curiously.

"Of course."

He smiled dryly and said, "Oliver seems to have all the luck."

"He won't, if you take Caroline away from him," she retorted a little sullenly.

He smiled at her.

"Don't you feel capable of consoling him?"

"Oh, Reid—please!" She put her hands over her face. "God, I wish I knew what was right. If it's really rather—rather a sudden business between Caroline and Oliver, and if she truly loved you, it makes a difference, of course. And I could make Oliver happy—I know I could—if only she were not there."

"You see?" He took hold of her hands and gently drew them down from her face, so that she had to look at him. "And *I* know that I could make *her* happy, if only your Oliver were not there. It's one of those rare occasions when the values—and the personalities—have got themselves hopelessly mixed. Don't you think we owe it to ourselves, and possibly to them too, to unmix things?"

"I—don't know. It sounds so plausible, of course. But its very plausibility makes me suspect it."

"Darling, you do make heavy weather of your own happiness, don't you?" he said amusedly.

"And you take things much too lightly," she cried accusingly. "You stand there calling me 'darling' and 'my sweet' and things like that, while you're supposed to be dying of love for another girl. It doesn't sound very——"

"Oh, no! Not dying of love," he assured her. "Very, very much alive and determined to fight for it. And as for calling you 'darling'—I think you *are* a darling, and I see no reason why I shouldn't put the thought into words occasionally."

She laughed vexedly, defeated by his unshakable good-humour.

"You have an answer for everything—like Satan," she declared.

"I hope you think the likeness ends there."

"I don't know." Leslie looked at him reflectively. "I've always thought Satan sounded attractive and full of vitality."

He laughed a good deal at that, and said it was no wonder he called her "darling" when she said such charming things. Whereupon Leslie suddenly realized just what she had said, and frowned and coloured a little.

"Well, let's leave this soul-searching for tonight," he suggested. "Tomorrow you may see things more as I do——"

"Or vice versa," she countered quickly.

He shook his head.

"No, my dear. I have my mind made up about this. But it's too late for us to pursue the discussion further. I'm sure you have a lot of courage and staying power, but today must have been a whale of a day for you, and if you're not feeling exhausted by now, you ought to be."

When he said that, Leslie became aware that she was indeed dead tired, in an excited, agitated way, and that, try as she would to look at the new problem in a fair and objective way, she simply could not do so. He was right. In all fairness they must break off the discussion now.

"You'd better go on ahead," she told him. "I know where the light-switches are."

But he smiled and said that if he were going to live there, the sooner he found out these things, the better.

So she went on ahead. And as he put out the lights, and came up the stairs behind her, she had the odd feeling that, in little or big things, one would very easily get into the habit of leaving responsibilities to Reid Carthay.

In the rather dim light of the upstairs landing, she looked at him with a flash of mischievous humour in her eyes and, because the rest of the household were probably asleep by now, it was in a whisper that she said to him,

"Do you do things for people because you're kind, or because you're arrogant?"

" 'Bossy' was the word you meant," he returned, also in a whisper. "And the answer is—neither. I do things only when I like people. Good night, my sweet." And he patted her cheek rather sharply and left her.

Leslie went into her own room, shut the door and leant against it. For almost a minute she made no attempt to put on the light. Only gazed almost absently round the palely moonlit room, while her mind drifted idly from point to point of her conversation with Reid Carthay.

Next day, when she was in the kitchen garden gathering peas, she saw Reid coming towards her with an air of purpose which suggested a deliberate seeking of her society, rather than any chance encounter. She went on rather deliberately with her task, but she experienced a little flutter of excited anticipation—not, she assured herself, because of anything in Reid's personality, but because one instinctively expected things to happen when he was around.

"Leslie——" He gathered a handful of pods and tossed them into her basket as a sort of token contribution. "There's something I want to ask you. I take it that—Oliver is more or less a friend of the family?"

"Oh, yes. Certainly."

"So that it would be quite in keeping with the general situation if you were to ring him up and suggested he brought his fiancée over here to meet the others?"

There was a moment's pause. Then she said,

"It would be quite a—likely proceeding, yes. But why should I? Do you think it would serve any useful purpose?"

"It would give the protagonists a chance to meet each other."

"Oh, Reid!"

"Well, we've got to meet sometime, you know. Don't you want to see what your rival—what Caroline—is like?"

She winced.

"Not—much. I'm a little afraid to see her."

"Hell! Why?" He evidently simply could not accept the idea of fearing to measure oneself against an adversary.

"Oh, Reid, I wish I had half your confidence," Leslie exclaimed, without actually answering his query.

"Nonsense. You're sweet as you are," he told her. "But take a grip on your courage and arrange for Oliver to bring her over here. It's probably your best and most painless way of meeting her, you know."

She knew reluctantly that he was right.

"Very well. But—when?"

"The first moment possible, of course!"

"This evening?"

"This evening would be fine."

"All right. I'll go and do it now." And she set down her basket and ran into the house, before her courage and resolution could fail her.

It was Oliver himself who answered her call, and he was obviously pleased at the idea of bringing Caroline to meet his old friends.

"She's staying here overnight," he explained. "I'll bring her to your place after dinner. Thanks, Leslie. It's a splendid idea. You think of everything."

She forbore to say that someone else had thought of this. Merely remarked, "That's all right, Oliver," in

56

what she grimly hoped was a sisterly tone, and replaced the receiver.

As she did so, Morley wheeled himself out into the hall. He must have heard her last few words, because he said,

"That was Oliver, was it?"

"Yes."

"He's engaged, Mother tells me."

"Yes. He is bringing her—bringing Caroline—over this evening, to meet us."

"Does he have to do that?" growled Morley.

"Oh, Morley! We're his oldest friends. I suggested he should bring her over."

"You did?" Morley looked at his sister, and his thin, rather haggard face softened. "No one can say you don't take your fences well, Leslie."

She wondered if she should say that Reid had urged her to take this particular fence. But it would involve too much explaining of what was best left alone, and would lead into the very debatable subject of her own exact motives in asking Oliver and his new fiancée to Cranley Magna. She contented herself with patting Morley's shoulder, smiling and saying,

"I'm not the most courageous member of this family. But I hope I'm not a bad loser."

He looked at her with anxious curiosity.

"Was it a bad shock, Leslie?"

"Say rather—a nasty jar," she retorted almost lightly. And she went back into the garden, marvelling to herself that she could conceal her inmost feelings from her brother, and yet reveal them to a comparative stranger.

"It's settled," she told Reid in a matter-of-fact voice.

"And don't pick any more peas, *please*. We have enough for a siege as it is."

He laughed.

"Sorry. I thought I'd better finish your job while you busied yourself about my affairs."

She looked at him reflectively.

"Would you say that telephone call was a question of your affairs or mine?"

He grinned.

"It's all in the way you look at it, I guess. What do you say?"

"I don't know. I wish I did," Leslie said, and took her peas away into the kitchen.

Outwardly she might appear extremely calm and matter-of-fact, but inwardly she felt frightened and agitated. Not only was there the direct ordeal of meeting Oliver's fiancée, and somehow making herself calmly accept the display of affection which he would presumably show for another girl, there was also the dreadful uncertainty in her own mind of what she meant to do.

Did she intend to stand by and watch Reid try to take Caroline away from Oliver? Or, rather—since there was nothing, it seemed, that she could do to influence Reid one way or the other—did she intend to keep a close watch on the situation and profit by it if she could?

Mentally she rejected the word "profit" as sounding too unscrupulous, and substituted the word "benefit." But she still felt uneasily that she was adopting the role of schemer, rather than good loser.

Only, if Caroline did turn to her first love, what sense would there be in Leslie not trying to console Oliver?

"It's all in the way one looks at it," she assured herself, unconsciously using Reid's own words. "Suppose I had been a good friend of Reid's and had never seen Oliver, I should feel quite differently. If I knew Reid had lost his girl through no fault of his own, I should be only too eager for him to win her back. And even if, in the intervening months, she had got herself entangled with someone else, I should still hope that Reid would regain her. I should be sorry for the other man, but I don't think I should rate his claim as high as Reid's."

It sounded wonderful, put that way. If only she had had no stake in the game herself!

"Am I being quite objective?" she asked herself

anxiously. "And if I am, and if I really think Reid has the better claim to Caroline, am I prepared even to help him get her back?"

But it was useless to pretend that she was still being objective when she reached that point in her reflections.

"I'm not being honest now!" she told herself ruthlessly. "But I have agreed to set the stage as Reid wants it this evening. Was *that* quite honest?"

Her common sense argued then that she had done nothing but arrange a perfectly harmless and ordinary family gathering. But her conscience would not let her entirely alone, and by the time the evening came she was sure that her conduct had not been entirely disinterested.

"It's funny we've never seen this Caroline Frenton before," remarked Alma. "You'd think Oliver would want to marry someone he *knew*, not a stranger."

"He probably feels he knows this girl now," Morley pointed out patiently.

"Oh, now—yes," Alma agreed. "But I mean you'd expect him to have married someone he'd known for ages, like Leslie or Kate."

"Much obliged," Katherine said. "I'm fond of Oliver, in a general, family way, but his Caroline may have him, for me."

Leslie smiled faintly, and even a little indulgently. But by no effort of will could she bring herself to second Katherine's sentiments.

"Oliver is our best friend, you know," Alma was busily explaining to Reid. "He lived quite near, and we've always known him. He's going to be a doctor, but he's living in Pencaster now, and I suppose that's where he met this Caroline."

"She is not, as you might suppose from my young sister's remarks, a camp-follower," Morley added. "She is apparently the niece of a perfectly reputable doctor in our nearest town."

"What did you say her name was?" Reid asked, so casually that Leslie could hardly suppress a smile of admiration.

"Caroline Frenton."

"Oh, then I know her already."

"You *do*?" Alma registered inordinate astonishment. "But what an extraordinary thing! Do you hear that, everyone? Reid knows this girl Oliver's going to marry."

There was a chorus of mild surprise, in which Leslie contrived to join convincingly. And Katherine added curiously,

"What is she like?"

"Dark, desirable, graceful, and with lots of oomph," replied Reid, with unexpected comprehensiveness.

There was a funny little silence, while they all registered this curiously vivid portrait of Caroline Frenton. Then Morley said reflectively,

"She doesn't sound Oliver's cup of tea, somehow."

"She may not be," Reid remarked amiably.

"But he's going to marry her," Alma protested in a shocked tone. And Leslie found herself saying severely,

"He sounded devoted to her when he told me about her."

But Reid merely smiled lazily and said, "Maybe, maybe."

And before Alma could voice any of the half-dozen questions which were obviously trembling on her lips, there were sounds of arrival in the hall, and a moment later Oliver came into the room in company with a girl whom they all recognized immediately under Reid's description of "dark, desirable, graceful and with lots of oomph."

In the first flurry of introductions, Leslie found, to her unutterable relief, that she was able to display complete self-control and a nice, impersonal pleasantness. But after a few moments, she found that her desire to sink into the background had been gratified beyond anything she had intended. In some curious way, she was overwhelmed by the personality of Caroline Frenton, and she had the peculiar, and most unwelcome, impression that her own colouring faded to something neutral and subdued beside the vivid drama of the other girl's looks.

Caroline was one of those people who naturally, and without either insistence or conceit, took the centre of the stage. No wonder Oliver had fallen for her! No wonder Reid hoped to win her back!

Leslie, in a fascinated, helpless way, found herself irresistibly assuming the identity of the sisterly, rather uninteresting friend who wished Oliver well without being of any particular importance in the scheme of things. She struggled against it. In that moment, she would have been gay and fast and a little outrageous, if she had known how to be. But Caroline held everyone's attention. And not until she fetched up before Reid, with a startled exclamation, did the spell of her enchanting invulnerability seem, momentarily, broken.

"Why, *Reid*! Where did you spring from?"

"France, darling. On a visit to my charming relations."

Immediately there was an outburst of explanations, in which Alma firmly took a leading part. Caroline contented herself with giving Reid a slow, pulse-disturbing smile, while she said to Oliver,

"He is one of my old flames, darling. But there's no need to call for pistols for two."

"I don't intend to." Oliver gave her an answering smile, which Katherine afterwards described as "besotted," and then turned on Reid an absent, indulgent glance of compassion which said as plainly as words that he was sorry for the poor fellow who was a backnumber, but had no intention of losing any sleep over him.

Oliver was talking energetically to Morley. But Caroline, who seemed able, in spite of her slightly lazy manner, to keep track of most that was going on around her, smilingly terminated her conversation with her host and drifted over to a seat nearer Leslie.

"Oliver has told me so much about you," she said, in a perfectly friendly tone. "I feel I know you better than the others, somehow."

"She's the easiest one to know. Aren't you, my sweet?" Reid said. And Leslie knew from his tone that he was looking down at her with an air which must be bordering on affectionate.

"Well, I wouldn't know about that." Leslie's voice was beautifully controlled, but her pulses leapt excitedly, for into the other girl's lazy, smiling eyes had come an entirely different expression. She was looking above Leslie's head at Reid now, and there was deliberate challenge in her face.

"And how do you spend *your* time, in this rural retreat?" she asked him, in an easy, mocking tone employed only between people who know each other very, very well.

"In the pleasantest way possible. Getting to know my cousins better," Reid assured her. "Especially this one." And to Leslie's amazement, amusement—and a little bit to her indignation too—she felt him drop a light, but unmistakable kiss on the top of her head.

For the life of her, she could not keep herself from glancing at the other girl, to see the effect on her, and she was a good deal startled to see Caroline's fine nostrils flare with some sudden emotion, and the line of her white teeth show for an instant on her lower lip.

Faintly embarrassed, Leslie looked quickly away again, and as she did so she encountered Oliver's astonished and angry gaze.

She gave a slight, audible gasp as, with a sort of breathless, icy exhilaration, she recognized something of the feelings which had prompted that expression. For the first time for days, Oliver had emerged from his happy bewilderment. And the shock which had accomplished that miracle was the disagreeable discovery that someone else apparently considered he had a right to be affectionately possessive towards a girl he had taken happily for granted all his life.

CHAPTER FIVE

LIKE all family parties where most of the people know each other well, this one kept on forming into little groups, disintegrating and regrouping, in a very informal way. And it was not long before Oliver detached himself quite naturally from his conversation with Morley and drifted casually into the group comprising Caroline, Leslie and Reid.

At first, Leslie thought he was seeking to rejoin his beloved, from whom he doubtless felt he had been separated long enough. But, after a minute or two, it dawned upon her that it was to her he wished to talk.

Caroline and Reid were getting on splendidly, in an exchange of gay and rapid cross-talk which kept things balanced on that curious knife-edge between intimacy and remoteness, only to be maintained when the protagonists are both amusing and quick-witted.

"Come and tell me how your parents are reacting to the new position, now they are getting used to it," Oliver said to Leslie, and, skilfully extricating her from the position of conversational buffer-state in which she had found herself, he drew her over to one of the deep window-seats, and sat down there with her.

As soon as they were established, however, in a reasonable degree of privacy, he seemed to forget his kind interest in her parents' welfare, because, without pressing the enquiry further, he looked across the room at Reid and said,

"So that's the fellow who has cut you all out with Great-Aunt Tabitha."

"Oh, that isn't quite how we feel about him, you know," Leslie protested, forgetting that this was exactly how they had felt about him twenty-four hours ago. "He is really very nice, and seems anxious to act in a most generous way."

Oliver was unimpressed.

"And what form does his generosity take?" he enquired, with a slight note of irony in his voice.

"He thinks Father should regard himself as morally entitled to some of the money at any rate, and he appears ready to go to a great deal of trouble to convince him of the fact."

"All of which entails his staying on at Cranley Magna for some time, I suppose."

"Naturally."

There was a rather pregnant silence. Then, without any finesse at all, Oliver said,

"I can't say I like his manner towards you."

"Why, Oliver——" Leslie was divided between amusement and a certain tenderness for him in his new found concern on her behalf. "He is very nice to me, I assure you."

Oliver frowned.

"Leslie, you mustn't take it amiss if I say that you girls are almost too sweet and naïve to keep certain types in their place. I mean, it's all very well for Morley and me to treat you with brotherly intimacy and—well, affection. But, hang it! that bounder's only known you since yesterday. What did he think he was doing, kissing your hair?"

Leslie bit her lip very hard. Mostly to keep herself from saying exactly what Reid *had* thought he was doing, kissing her hair. And a very successful manoeuvre it appeared to have been too.

"He doesn't mean anything serious, Oliver. He's very free and easy in his manner, I know, because——"

"Much too free and easy."

"He regards himself as more or less of a relation."

"Nonsense." Oliver seemed more annoyed than soothed by this view. "Does he regard himself as more or less of a relation of Caroline's too?"

A little startled by the change of attack, Leslie glanced quickly across to where Caroline and Reid were still sparring enjoyably.

"Well——" she began, seeking for words to reassure Oliver, without actually descending to an untruth.

But she had no need to worry, for he went on immediately,

"Not that Caroline isn't well able to look after herself." He smiled reminiscently, and something of his natural good-humour returned. "I don't worry about her. She can take the measure of anyone, and she has evidently handled him well before."

"Ye-es," murmured Leslie, overwhelmed with astonishment that Caroline should awake no protective feelings in Oliver, while she herself, for the first time in their joint existence, seemed to strike him as someone in need of support and advice.

"It's you I'm worried about," Oliver went on, with a degree of earnestness which might, perhaps, have been called brotherly but certainly transcended anything Morley would have presumed to display on her behalf.

"You really don't need to worry, Oliver!" Leslie was beginning to grow restive in her role of foolish, unprotected innocent. "Believe me, I am perfectly capable of managing Reid Carthay—or anyone else, come to that."

As she said the words, she knew they were strictly not true. Managing Reid Carthay—though in a sense other than that in Oliver's mind—had proved beyond her once or twice already.

"Well, my dear, of course I don't want to interfere," said Oliver, who quite obviously did. "But, as you know, I've a good deal of brotherly——" He stopped, as though suddenly discovering something which surprised him. "Well, no, 'brotherly' isn't quite the word, I suppose. But, anyway, I've always regarded you girls as very much my concern, and particularly you, Leslie. You must forgive me if I was taking a bit too much on myself. But what I wanted to say was that you'd better keep this so-called cousin at a distance, and if you have any sort of trouble with him, just let me know."

"Thank you, Oliver. I will," Leslie promised rather meekly. "But I really don't expect any trouble."

"Then don't encourage him," Oliver retorted, with

an unusual spurt of irritation. And he seemed a good deal surprised when Leslie laughed.

Oliver and she stayed for about an hour. And when they had taken their leave, the Greeves, in the manner of families, immediately embarked on a delightful, though not unkindly, inquest on the newcomer.

Aware as she was of Reid's particular place in things, Leslie felt rather uncomfortable for the first few minutes. But she very soon realized that she was worrying herself unduly. It would have taken much more than a gaggle of Greeves to disconcert Reid Carthay.

"She's very good-looking," remarked Alma—always quickest off the mark when it came to personalities.

"She's exactly as Reid described her," replied Morley.

"You must have known her very well, Reid." Katherine glanced at him in idle curiosity.

"Reasonably well," Reid agreed, but seemed otherwise disinclined to join in the discussion.

"I mean—it was clever of you to describe her right away so accurately and in so few words."

"A very beautiful and attractive girl," remarked Richard Greeve at that moment, in a tone which silenced all other comment. "I am just a little surprised that she took anyone so—ordinary as our good Oliver."

And, with this final and rather depressing dictum on Oliver, Richard Greeve made his exit.

Leslie looked after him with a vexed laugh. But Morley said,

"For once, I'm rather in agreement with Papa, I think. I also am a little surprised that she took Oliver. And as I said before, I don't think she sounds—and I don't think she is—Oliver's cup of tea either."

"Then perhaps this will be one of those cases when there is a slip between cup and lip," Reid suggested lightly. "Coming into the garden for a breath of air, Leslie?"

Part of her—the responsible, conscientious part of her—very much wanted to refuse. But although she despised herself for wanting to talk things over with him, Leslie could not, for anything, have resisted the

66

urge to hear what Reid had to say when none of the others were by.

She nodded in a casual, friendly way, and they went out together into the warm dusk.

For the first few minutes they strolled in silence, each perhaps intending that the other should start the conversation. Then he said reflectively—almost softly, "I'd forgotten how beautiful she is."

"Forgotten!"

"Oh, only in the final, sharpest sense. I had a clear picture of her in my mind, of course. But no mental recollection ever really supplies that final glow of colour or clarity of outline. It's like having a beautiful lamp, without the light inside."

"Yes. I know what you mean. You're still—very much in love with her, aren't you, Reid?"

"Lord, yes! Sometimes I wish I weren't. But there'll never be any other girl for me."

"Even—if you don't get her?"

"I shall get her, Leslie."

She held her breath for a moment and tried to steady the beating of her heart.

"Was it something that happened this evening which makes you so sure of that, Reid?"

He didn't answer her at first, but seemed to follow his own thoughts on some rather dark path. Then his attention came back to her with a start and he said,

"What did you say? Yes, of course. Everything that happened this evening. She isn't for him, my sweet." He was in his characteristic, half-mocking mood of self-confidence again. "And she knows it as well as I do. It won't take so very much to make her think again."

"And what about Oliver?" Leslie enquired rather flatly.

"Oliver?" Reid laughed suddenly and rather shamelessly. "Oh, he's restive and possessive about you already. Did you see the way he looked when I kissed you?"

"Yes. I did. And you ought to have been ashamed

of yourself, Reid. It was taking things too far."

"Nonsense! Did he say so?"

"He did, as a matter of fact."

Reid gave a shout of laughter. Triumphant laughter.

"What did I tell you? Fate unkindly mixed up the characters in this little drama, and all we have to do is unmix them. Oliver is already wishing irritably that he had the right to protect you from my attentions."

"Reid!" She was half vexed, half amused. "That doesn't alter the fact that he is, at this moment, very much in love with Caroline."

"Every man is in love with Caroline when he first knows her," Reid declared carelessly. "Even your father felt romantic stirrings when she smiled at him."

Leslie's reluctant laugh admitted the probable truth of that. But aloud she only said,

"That would make her rather an uncomfortable person to be married to, I should have thought."

"Divine discomfort," Reid countered easily. "But, allow me to say, a discomfort which I could tackle very much better than your Oliver."

"I suppose you are right." She glanced at Reid in the faint evening light and, seeing the brilliant, wicked smile which he gave, she thought she could well imagine that he could manage even Caroline.

"Reid," she said almost timidly. "How—I mean, what——"

"You mean—what is the next move?" he prompted her airily. "Though you are rather too nice a girl to choose your wording to sound as though you're scheming."

She pressed her lips together.

"Well," she said at last, "let's be honest before everything. What *is* the next move?" And she paused to pick a withered flower-head from one of the rose bushes.

"I think," he said, pausing beside her, "that the next move is for you to become engaged to me."

She straightened up and looked at him.

"What did you say?"

"Just exactly what you thought I said, sweetheart. And don't tell me that you don't know what on earth I am talking about, because of course you do."

She was completely silent, all her protests and indignant denials dying on her lips.

"You mean," she said slowly at last, "that the shock of seeing you apparently belonging to someone else is all that is needed to make her realize it's you she wants?"

"I was thinking a little of Oliver too," he replied modestly. "How do you think he will take the news of your engagement to me?"

"Oh!" For a moment she saw again Oliver's disturbed, dissatisfied face as he warned her against allowing Reid too many liberties. "He'll—I mean, he would just hate it."

"A healthy bit of hate," remarked Reid in an amused tone.

"Reid, sometimes you terrify me, with your ruthlessness about what you want and your confidence that you're right!"

"And you," he said, laughing a little and putting his arm round her, "are much too timid for this job. Don't endow other people with your own delicacies and scruples. You're sweet, and I wouldn't change you for the world. But can't you see that Caroline and I are much more violent, ruthless, earthy creatures than you are?"

"I wasn't thinking of you and Caroline so much," she said rather faintly. "I was thinking of Oliver."

"Well, then, Oliver, I suppose, is much more your own kind. Don't you think you ought to rescue him from Caroline?" And he laughed softly and kissed the tip of her ear.

She was completely still. So still that he drew her back lightly against him without any resistance on her part. For a few moments they were silent. Then he realized suddenly that she was crying. Not stormily, as she had wept the previous day, but quietly, with the tears slipping rather helplessly down her cheeks.

"Leslie, don't!" He was surprised, and a good deal dismayed, and on a sudden impulse he gathered her in his arms as though she were a child. "What's the matter, sweetheart? I didn't mean to tease you as far as that. What's wrong?"

She hid her face against his shoulder for a moment, and was understood to say that she hated herself.

"Yourself? Oh, no!" he exclaimed in amused protest. "Really, that's terribly illogical of you. You can hate me, if you like, or Caroline, or even Oliver. But not yourself. You're much the nicest person in this set-up."

"Oh, I'm *not*!" She dried her eyes on the handkerchief he offered her, and gave a faint smile of protest. "I—I hardly know myself, ever since I learned that Oliver didn't love me after all. I don't seem to have any—any dignity or decency or proper standards at all. I couldn't have believed that I'd even entertain the idea of faking an engagement with one man, to make myself more desirable to another. And yet, when you talk to me about it——"

"I know—I'm a plausible scoundrel," he said regretfully, and smiled at her.

"No, you're not." To her own great astonishment, she put up her hand and just touched his cheek. "You're bold and perhaps a bit ruthless and cruelly realistic. But I don't think you're a scoundrel. You honestly think you have the greater claim on Caroline, don't you?"

"Sure." He was watching her rather closely.

"I *think* I think so too."

"Come, that's something."

"And I do honestly believe that, in the long run, I could probably make Oliver happier than she could. Though of course it's terribly easy to deceive oneself over anything that matters so much."

"Terribly. But I'm sure you're right there," he said, smiling.

She paused, as though unwilling to follow the line of

70

argument further. But, characteristically, he cleared the next fence for her.

"In fact," he said, "you agree about the probability of its being generally desirable that I should marry Caroline, and Oliver should marry you, even if we argue from the highest motives. What really worries you is the idea of our achieving that by a bit of light-hearted deception."

"Light-hearted?" She looked at him with rather shadowed eyes, and queried the word a little reproachfully.

"Certainly. Don't you think you could rather enjoy being engaged to me on a purely temporary basis? If we do this thing at all, we may as well enjoy it."

"I haven't said I will do it," she whispered hastily.

"No."

He did not elaborate on that, as though willing to let her make up her own mind in the final analysis. And then he was so still that she had the curious impression that he was like a bird-watcher, who feared to make the slightest movement lest he should frighten away something he thought almost within his grasp.

"Reid—how long would we have to—keep it up?"

"What, darling?"

He bent his head down to hers, because her question had been so low that it was almost impossible to catch.

She repeated the words, curiously aware of a nearness which was not only physical.

"The engagement? Not very long, I imagine."

"And then, when it had served its purpose, it could be—dissolved quite easily."

"Of course."

"I wish I didn't feel so—mean about it. As though my one thought were to take away the girl Oliver wants."

"Dear heart, you won't take her away, if she truly loves him. Remember, if Oliver is the man she wants, your being engaged to me won't make me any the more desirable to her."

"No, that's true." Leslie glanced up with a relieved smile. "It's only a sort of—of test."

"If you like to put it that way."

She thought she did like to put it that way and, though she drew a long sigh, a much more satisfied and contented look came into her face.

He watched her, with a sort of indulgent amusement.

"Well, when do we announce the engagement?"

"Oh——" Her glance came quickly to his face again then. "We shall have to do *some* leading up to it, Reid. After all, I only met you yesterday."

"Don't you think I might have swept you off your feet?"

She smiled and said, "No." But in her heart she thought he probably was the sort who swept one off one's feet.

"Perhaps the real argument is that I'm not the kind to *be* swept off my feet," she said. "Give me a few days, Reid."

"Whatever you say. But don't make it too long."

"I promise," she said rather soberly. And they went back into the house together.

Only Morley and Katherine were still in the drawing-room and, glancing round, Leslie asked absently,

"Where's Alma?"

"Why, gone to bed, of course. Long ago." Katherine looked at her curiously. And only then did it dawn on Leslie that she and Reid had been out in the garden a very long time, and that both her brother and sister looked a little oddly at her because of it.

"I didn't realize it was so late," she said, and felt a certain embarrassed annoyance that she should have put herself in that position. Then she realized that, quite unwittingly, she had planted the first interested sense of query in their minds, and she supposed she ought to be glad of it.

She went and sat by Morley, and asked him in a low voice how he was feeling, because once or twice during that harassing evening she had thought he looked more than ordinarily pale and drawn, and her anxiety returned in full force now that she saw him directly under the light.

He put down his book and smiled at her.

"Not too good. But not too awful either."

"What about having Dr. Bendick look in tomorrow?"

"He's going to. There's a specialist coming down from London too."

"Morley!" She was overwhelmed by remorseful anxiety, and her own affairs were completely forgotten. "Is there something wrong?"

"Not more so than usual. Don't get excited."

"But I didn't know anything about this."

"It was necessary. Oliver arranged it all. He told me this evening that it was all fixed."

"You mean that you've been feeling lately that you're in need of more—of different treatment? Haven't you been as well as usual, Morley?"

"No. There's been a slow deterioration and——"

"Oh, why didn't you tell me, dear?" she exclaimed in a tone of loving concern.

Morley smiled at her.

"Because you girls get in a fearful flap over nothing," he countered with brotherly candour. "Besides, we've none of us exactly needed something extra to worry over lately. There was nothing you could have done, Leslie, even if you'd known. Except worry—and I'd rather you didn't do that. I only told you now because you're bound to know about the specialist tomorrow, and it might be a bit of a shock if I'd said nothing in advance. But he's supposed to be a splendid man—Sir James Trevant—and old Bendick seems to think he might not only be able to deal with the present trouble, but even perhaps do more for me than anyone's managed to do before. So, for heaven's sake, look on the bright side, and don't think that the mere arrival of a specialist means something disastrous."

Leslie paused when she reached the top of the stairs, because she saw that the light was still on in her mother's room, and the idea came to her that perhaps her mother most of all would need convincing whenever she declared her new-found passion for Reid. After all, to her mother she had been frankest about her feelings for Oliver. It was going to be rather difficult to reverse all that in so short a time.

Leslie knocked on the door and, in answer to the rather subdued "Come in," she entered.

Her mother was not in bed. She was standing by her dressing-table and, as Leslie came in, she turned upon her daughter a face which bore faint but unmistakable traces of tears.

"Why, Mother, what is it? What are you doing?"

Leslie came quickly across the room. But she fetched up short before the dressing-table and, silent in her turn, she stared down at what was spread out there.

A pretty, old-fashioned jewel-case stood open, and half its contents were spilled out, as though an eager hand had turned them over and rejected them. There was nothing there of genuine value. Only—in that most pathetic of phrases—of sentimental value. And even as Leslie gazed down at the pretty little oddments with a suddenly tightened throat, her mother said,

"They aren't worth much, I'm afraid—not any of them. Except to me. There's my engagement ring, of course——" She turned it nervously on her delicate hand. But Leslie broke in almost sharply because she was so moved,

"Don't be silly, Mother dear. We haven't reached the point of having to sell your jewellery yet. Whatever made you think of it?"

"Morley."

"You don't mean he said something——"

"No, of course not! But he's very ill, you know, Leslie. Much more ill than any of us realized. I spoke to Dr. Bendick half an hour ago on the telephone, when you were out in the garden. He thinks almost certainly that Morley will need immediate and expensive treatment—possibly even an operation."

"I—didn't know." Nervously and absently, Leslie fingered the trinkets in her turn. "But didn't Reid tell Father that he wanted help? That he thought——"

"Morley wouldn't have it."

"But of course he would! How ridiculous!"

"He's very proud, Leslie. In the way injured people are sometimes proud. It's as though they can't help making more difficulties for themselves. He regards Reid as a stranger. He wouldn't take money from a stranger."

"But Reid isn't that! He's a relation—well, almost a relation."

"Oh, no, dear." Her mother shook her head sadly. "We all repudiated that relationship when it didn't mean any advantage to us. Morley isn't the one to accept it now, just because we need money. Your father will be much easier to convince than Morley."

"It's absurd to call Reid a stranger, Mother," Leslie reiterated almost angrily. "He doesn't even *feel* like one. He—he seems like one of the family."

Her mother smiled faintly but protestingly.

"I only wish he did, Leslie. I only wish he *were* one of us. I know I shocked you yesterday when I said I wished Katherine would fall in love with him and marry him. But when I think what it would mean to have him for a son-in-law, I can hardly keep myself from asking Kate if she doesn't rather like him, after all."

"Oh——" Leslie said. Then she looked at the coral brooch she had absently picked up, and she felt her colour rise as she forced a protesting smile to her lips. "Please don't say anything like that to Kate——"

"Oh, I shouldn't really!"

"—It makes me feel a little—jealous."

"Jealous, Leslie! Of whom, my dear? I don't understand."

Leslie laughed nervously. And the nervousness was genuine, if the laughter was not.

"Why does Kate have to be the only one cast for the role? Why shouldn't I be considered too?"

"You, my dear?" But I thought—— You told me——"

"Oh, Mother, I don't know really what's come over me," Leslie cried, with enough genuine fervour to make that ring true. "But—aren't people sometimes swept off their feet?"—Reid's useful phrase. "Can't you imagine that Reid might seem—seem overwhelmingly attractive to some girls? I mean—crazily attractive. To the exclusion of everyone else."

"Yes," her mother said slowly. "I can imagine exactly that. Only I shouldn't have expected it to happen with you."

"Nor should I," Leslie said breathlessly. "But he asked me to marry him just now, Mother. And I—said I would."

"Leslie! Because you felt you should, or because you wanted to?"

"Because I wanted to. Because I love him," Leslie said with complete recklessness.

And then her mother sat down and cried tears of such aching relief that Leslie could only stand and stare at her in unutterable dismay.

CHAPTER SIX

"DON'T, Mother," Leslie said at last. "Don't cry like that. It isn't necessary. I—I thought you would consider my news good news."

"But I do, darling!" Her mother dried her eyes and managed a pale smile. "You mustn't think I'm unhappy. I was crying with relief, I think. Relief and—and a sort of dismay that it can mean so much to me that my daughter should marry a rich man. Oh, Leslie, are you sure?"

"Sure that he's going to marry me?" Leslie smiled faintly in her turn.

"No, no! Sure that you love him. But how can you be, in so short a time? It's absurd even to talk of it. But do you feel truly that you will love him? It's not just that marrying him would be such a wonderful, wonderful solution of our troubles?"

"I'm not marrying him for his money, Mother, if you want my categorical assurance of that."

"I can hardly believe it." Her mother clasped her thin hands together and smiled less uncertainly this time. "Even Morley couldn't resent help from his brother-in-law."

"No," Leslie said, and suddenly her lips went dry. For, in her eagerness to convince her mother, she had overplayed her part—laid the emphasis where no emphasis was due.

The term "brother-in-law" had roused her to a realization of the hollowness of the comfort she was urging upon her mother. Engaged to Reid she might be, for so long or short a time as was necessary to bring Caroline to her senses. But there was no question of a marriage.

Impossible to draw that delicate distinction for her mother. But Leslie could already see the complications ahead, already visualize the cruel disappointment which must follow on the false hopes she was raising.

"Well, I can't help it," she thought desperately. "Let Mother take what comfort she can from it while it lasts. I suppose I can come to some sort of arrangement with Reid. *I* have no pride where Morley's good is concerned. If anyone could make Morley well, I'd be satisfied to have Reid pay, in any identity—my fiancé, my husband-to-be—anything."

Aloud, she said, "Go to bed, Mother dear. You don't need to worry any more. Everything is going to be all right—you'll see."

Her mother kissed her lovingly.

"Leslie darling, you know I wouldn't have you sacrifice your own happiness, even to give Morley the best chance in the world, don't you? But if, in a little while, when you've given yourself some time to think things over, you are sure you love Reid, then nothing would make me happier. It isn't only because of what it will mean to all of us, I think he'd make any woman he loved very happy."

"Do you, Mother?" Leslie smiled as she returned her mother's kiss, but she spoke a little too absently, too impersonally for a girl who had just fallen in love. "I wonder what makes you sure of that?"

"Reid himself, I suppose." Her mother looked reflective. "He could make one *un*happy too, I am sure, because of his obstinacy and his ruthlessness. But there's an underlying generosity of spirit to which one could always appeal. If he truly loves you, you would be—safe with him, Leslie. I know that."

"I'm—sure of it," Leslie said, but again there was that slight nervous laugh.

"But all the same, dear, think a little longer before you become actually engaged."

"Oh, no——" Leslie, who was at the door, turned quickly for a last word. "No, Mother. He is set on our announcing our engagement as quickly as possible. I—I want that too."

And then she went away, before her mother could say more, aware that she had burnt her boats with a

78

speed and thoroughness beyond anything she had intended.

She thought of seeking out Reid, late though it now was, and telling him that they were already completely committed to their faked engagement. But she suddenly felt so limp and so emotionally weary that she knew she could handle no more scenes of this sort. Certainly no scenes with anyone of Reid's vitality and exuberance.

Tomorrow would be soon enough to tell him. Tomorrow would be soon enough to enter on the dangerous piece of make-believe which they had undertaken.

In spite of a restless night, Leslie was up early and, having already seen from her window that Reid was out in the garden, she went downstairs and out into the bright morning air.

"Reid——" She came up with him, where he was standing watching, with a good deal of amusement, the indefatigable labours of a large striped spider.

"Hello, there." He threw a casual, friendly glance at her. "Come and look at this fellow. If we carry out our intentions with half his persistence we shan't do badly."

"Aren't spiders usually supposed to be 'she'?" Leslie said. But she came up and stood beside him.

"You're probably right at that." He grinned, though he did not take his eyes off the spider. "That probably accounts for the persistence. I'm going to rely a lot on you in the coming weeks."

"You may," she said quietly, and he glanced at her quickly.

"You haven't changed your mind, eh?" He smiled and drew her arm through his.

"On the contrary, I've already made a good beginning with the job of telling the family."

"Good God!" His admiration was unmistakable that time. "And did they believe you?"

"Certainly they believed me."

"I'm a little surprised that they should."

"Oh, no. In Morley's case, it was only a question of accepting a first suspicion of the truth—I mean of what we wanted him to think the truth. And in

79

Mother's case——" She stopped, and then her voice dropped a little as she said, "Mother so terribly *wanted* to believe, poor darling!"

"Because of your father?"

"No. Because of Morley," Leslie said. And then told him what her mother had told her the previous evening.

He listened in silence. Then he said,

"You know I will do everything he will let me do, don't you?"

It was almost matter of fact in its simplicity and its completeness, this undertaking of his. And suddenly she found herself remembering what her mother had said about his having an underlying generosity of spirit.

She pressed Reid's arm with more intimacy and gratitude than she knew.

"It isn't incumbent on you, you know. Mother said that Morley probably would accept help from his brother-in-law. But you and I know that you'll never really be in that position."

"Hell! What does that matter?" Reid retorted with careless impatience. "I've been trying to hand back some of this damned money to your family ever since I acquired it. Don't spoil a good opportunity by saying it doesn't really exist."

Leslie laughed softly. She was beginning to know by now that even when he swore it usually meant either that he was moved or in high good-humour. She could not imagine that he ever swore in temper.

"Mother says you have an underlying generosity of spirit," she said thoughtfully. "I think I see what she means."

"Nonsense." He spoke a little roughly. "I usually get a good return for anything I do."

She looked scepitcal and, for some reason, a trifle amused.

"Is that so? What return are you expecting for helping Morley?"

"Well, you're obliging me pretty handsomely, aren't you?"

"By becoming engaged to you? I thought that was for our mutual pleasure and advantage."

He laughed reluctantly, gave her an odd glance and said,

"I don't know you in this mood."

"No," Leslie said with a slight sigh. "I don't know myself very well either. Perhaps I'm demonstrating that Oliver was wrong when he declared I was too nice and naïve to keep a man like you in his place."

"He said that? The man's a fool," Reid declared contemptuously.

Leslie flushed and pulled her arm away, indescribably annoyed by this insult to Oliver.

"He is nothing of the sort! And he knows me a great deal better than you ever will," she cried angrily.

"Then he should know that you could manage most men with one hand tied behind you," was the astonishing thing Reid said.

"You—think that?" Her anger was quenched in her surprise, and, to tell the truth, in a peculiar feeling of gratification too.

"Of course," he said, but a little disagreeably for him. "Shall we go in and receive the family's congratulations?"

"If you like." They turned and strolled towards the house together. "But Mother may not have told them yet."

"Then we will tell them."

The family were already gathered at the breakfast table when they came in, Morley's place only being empty. And when Leslie saw the ceremonious air with which her father rose to address her, she realized that he at least needed no telling.

"My dear, this is wonderful news," he began.

But his wife caught his arm and said urgently, "Richard, I told you Leslie may not want it to be public property yet."

"We don't mind," Reid said, with a smile at her.

"What isn't to be public property?" demanded Alma,

who had preternaturally acute hearing where semi-secrets were concerned.

"Dear Leslie and Reid——"

"If I may be allowed to make my voice heard," boomed Richard Greeve in rich, but slightly sulky, tones, because he was annoyed at having his speech of congratulations mangled like this, "I should like to congratulate my dear daughter"—he put a paternal hand on Leslie's shoulder—"and my good friend Reid" —by reaching rather uncomfortably far he was able to clap his other hand on Reid's shoulder—"on their engagement. I can only say that it is a marriage that will give me the very greatest happiness and satisfaction."

The news of Leslie's engagement, viewed through the rosy spectacles of Alma and her father, proved something of an antidote to the news about Morley—broken now for the first time to Alma and Katherine. But afterwards Leslie's elder sister caught her by the arm and drew her into one of the window alcoves, and demanded with some urgency,

"You aren't marrying Reid in order to repair the family fortunes, are you?"

"No, of course not, Kate. Why should you think so?"

"Well, you know we did talk over the idea of acquiring rich husbands a night or two ago."

Leslie laughed.

"And you didn't show any signs of being shocked by the prospect then," Leslie reminded her. "In fact, you were rather frank about your plans for yourself."

"Oh, for *myself*—yes," Katherine agreed almost naïvely. "But you're made for something different. I don't think you'd be happy, Leslie, if you married for anything but love."

"Well, I'm marrying for love," Leslie retorted. And she spoke with a sudden fierceness, so that Katherine fell back, almost literally, in surprise, and somehow found herself unable to continue the discussion.

It was an anxious, uncertain day, until Dr. Bendick and the specialist should have come and given their verdict on Morley. Leslie particularly, consumed with loving care for her brother, found it increasingly difficult to remember that she was also supposed to be the happy, newly-engaged girl, with sweet distractions to temper her sisterly anxiety.

Only Reid's watchfulness and, to tell the truth, his tact kept her from giving herself away on more than one occasion. He did also offer her some very real comfort when he heard who the specialist was whom Dr. Bendick had summoned.

"Oh, Trevant is reckoned to be almost a miracle-man at his job," he assured Leslie confidently. "Do you mean to say you've never heard or read about him?"

"Only to remember the name. Is he *really* so good, Reid?"

"He has a tremendous reputation—both as a personality and as a surgeon. A very handsome man, you know—rather like an elderly film star from all accounts—and something of a show-off. But a genius. Even his most jealous rivals concede him that."

When Sir James Trevant arrived, Leslie caught a glimpse of him before he was taken into Morley's room, and the little she saw confirmed much of what Reid had said. The famous surgeon was a tall, handsome, picturesque figure. But there was about him also that indefinable aura of success and calm confidence which belongs only to the man who *knows* he cannot fail.

Even so, Leslie remained in a state of nervous suspense, and she passionately wished it were she, rather than her parents, who would have a chance of speaking to him afterwards. Would her mother, in her anxious diffidence, or her father in his pompous attitudinizing, make it perfectly clear that no expense was to be spared in the effort to make Morley better?

"The ideal would be, of course, to have Morley removed to Trevant's own nursing home for a few months," Dr. Bendick said after Sir James had left. "But—I don't know——" He fondled his chin meditatively and looked round sympathetically on his old friends, with an expression which showed plainly that Oliver had told him of their recent reverse.

"Then please make the arrangements as soon as possible."

It was Reid who spoke, and Dr. Bendick swung round in his chair to regard him.

Mrs. Greeve murmured a belated introduction, and her husband, in the tone of one who endorsed what his personal representative had said, remarked,

"To be sure. Let the arrangements be made as soon as possible."

Leslie saw the faintest grim smile lift the corners of Reid's mouth. But he emphasized his own words with an authoritative little nod to Dr. Bendick, and the doctor, rising with an extremely satisfied look, prepared to take his leave.

Mrs. Greeve then remembered social and friendly obligations, and charmingly expressed their pleasure and congratulation on Oliver's engagement.

"Well, I don't know, I don't know. I suppose young people always think they know their own minds best," Dr. Bendick said a little obscurely.

Whereupon Richard Greeve, unable to resist the temptations of family competition even in the matter of engagements, smiled indulgently and remarked,

"We too have had our share of surprises in this line. Our dear Leslie"—she had never been more dear to him—"presented us this morning with a *fait accompli.* She is engaged to our young friend here."

Dr. Bendick, like most elderly experienced practitioners, was a shrewd man and a close observer of human nature. If his son's engagement had surprised—and a little disappointed—him, Leslie's engagement quite obviously astounded and troubled him.

Instead of offering the congratulations which Richard Greeve evidently expected, he frowned at Leslie and said bluntly,

"Very sudden, isn't it, Leslie? What's the idea?"

"These things *are* sudden, my good friend," declared his host genially, clapping him on the shoulder, because that was one of his favourite ways of displaying congratulation and pleasure. "We mustn't let ourselves grow too old to remember that, you know."

Dr. Bendick glanced at his neighbour as though he thought him a likeable ass, which he did. But to the girl he had hoped to have as his daughter-in-law he repeated,

"Isn't this rather too sudden—too impulsive?"

"I don't think so." Leslie managed to smile at him, though she knew he was much more difficult to deceive than her parents. "I know it seems like that. But as—as Father says, it sometimes does happen that way."

A little shaken by this encounter, Leslie found she very much disliked the prospect of having to give her news to Morley and submit to what she guessed would be the most searching cross-examination of all. This, at least, she told herself suddenly, she would delegate to someone else, and as the door closed behind Dr. Bendick she turned impulsively to her mother.

"Mother, will you tell Morley about Reid and me? I don't expect he ought to have many visitors or much excitement today. You'll be able to judge the best time and the—the best way of telling him."

Her mother, knowing how close Leslie and Morley were, looked surprised.

"Don't you think he'd rather hear from you yourself, darling?"

"No." She was emphatic in her sudden nervousness. "I don't want to explain and—and argue any more. I want just to—enjoy my engagement."

"She wants to come with me and buy her ring, Mrs. Greeve," Reid remarked carelessly, for he, probably more than her mother, had sensed the note of nervous strain in Leslie's voice. "I'm going to run her over to Pencaster in my car this afternoon, so that she can choose what she likes."

"Oh——" began Leslie, rather startled.

But the small exclamation was lost in the smiling, indulgent emphasis with which her mother said,

"Why, of course! Enjoy yourself, darling, and don't

worry about Morley. I'll tell him. You go and have every bit of pleasure you can. I don't want you to remember this as a day of anxiety. It's a day of great rejoicing too."

"Thank you," Leslie said softly. And for a moment the difference between reality and romantic deception weighed on her so heavily that she felt the tears come into her eyes.

The moment she and Reid were alone together, she exclaimed,

"I don't know that I meant to force things as far as this!"

"As far as what?" He looked surprised.

"Oh, a ring and—and everything."

He laughed in good-humoured derision.

"There's woman's logic for you! You haven't winced over the boldest measures, and now you shy at a little thing like a ring."

"It's not a little thing, Reid. It's a—a symbol."

"Well, come along and let's find you the handsomest symbol we can," he returned, unmoved.

And presently Leslie found herself beside him in his car—with a fleeting thought for how much had happened since she last sat there—driving through the alternating showers and sunlight to Pencaster.

Reid, as she had expected, proved well able to find exactly what he sought with the minimum of fuss.

Leslie thought she remembered hearing once that "diamonds always command their value." And so, with the vague idea of ensuring Reid against too heavy a loss when the ring had to be returned, she chose a diamond ring, with a light but curiously beautiful setting.

"Like it?" he asked with a smile, when it was safely on her finger.

"Very much," Leslie assured him.

But a few minutes later she saw him glance at it restlessly and a little moodily, and she supposed he was thinking, not unnaturally, how much rather he would have put it on another girl's hand. To be confident of the success of one's little escapade was one thing. To enjoy the counterfeit of what should have been a cherished reality was very much something else.

On the whole, she felt sorry for Reid in that moment.

He took her out to tea, and she realized, rather to her amusement, that they found each other good company. Not that they had a great deal in common, she supposed. At least, not in their special interests, or their way of looking at life.

But perhaps having so few secrets from each other made a difference. They had been so ruthlessly frank with each other, stripping every bit of romantic or even social pretence from their relationship. What was left was a good-humoured, half-cynical understanding of each other which made conversation remarkably refreshing and simple.

When she came to think of it, each probably knew more of the other than anyone else of their acquaintance.

It was a sobering thought, that. To imagine that this smiling, confident half-stranger sitting opposite her knew more of her inmost thoughts and feelings than her own mother did—or her brother or sisters, or the man she really loved.

"It's an odd relationship," she said aloud.

He raised his eyebrows and smiled at her, but made no pretence of not understanding her.

"Rather satisfying though," he countered consideringly. To which she agreed, with a half-reluctant laugh.

And then Caroline came into the restaurant, and right up to their table and almost past them before she realized that they were there.

"Hello, you two!" She paused, her slow beautiful smile in evidence, but her big dark eyes widening, as Reid rose to his feet to greet her with careless friendliness. "What brought you here?"

"We—drove into Pencaster to have tea," Leslie said a little quickly, because she flinched suddenly before the final dramatic disclosure.

"We drove into Pencaster to buy an engagement ring," amended Reid good-humouredly. "Leslie and I have just got engaged."

Leslie watched, fascinated, as the lazy calm of Caroline's usual expression splintered before her eyes. Just for a moment she saw the dark, strong currents of emotion which ran below the usually unruffled surface, and she was not quite sure if she were frightened or elated or apprehensive.

Then Caroline, with a tremendous effort, regained her normal expression, and in a voice which hardly even trembled she said,

"Engaged? But you can't be. Oh, no, really that's quite impossible."

CHAPTER SEVEN

THE COOL reasonableness of the tone in which Caroline uttered her objection to their engagement shook Leslie. It seemed to imply that she was about to produce some overriding argument which would reduce to absurdity the very idea of such an engagement — real or fictitious.

But if Leslie's sense of security crumbled, Reid's showed itself cheerfully impervious to this form of attack. On the contrary, it was he who reduced Caroline's objection to absurdity by saying,

"My dear, incredulous Caroline, it is not only possible, but an accomplished fact. There is no known cause or just impediment, you know," and for a moment his eyes glittered dangerously. "Why should you think an engagement between Leslie and me so impossible?"

She was shaken in her turn.

"It's so sudden — such short notice." She was still standing by the table, having brushed aside Reid's invitation to join them, and her glance drifted puzzledly over Leslie, as though seeking to find in her some explanation of the inexplicable.

Leslie withstood the glance admirably, and said quite gently,

"*I* feel as though it's very sudden and almost unbelievable too. But that doesn't make it any less — less wonderful."

She thought for a moment that she had overplayed her part. The breathless way she had said "wonderful," for instance, sounded almost touching, even to her own ears.

But Reid seemed well satisfied.

"You see, my dear," he said pleasantly to Caroline. "I think you are answered."

It was not in Caroline to be completely routed. She remained for a minute or two, offering cool congratulations now, and asking perfunctory questions, such as when were they going to be married?

"Soon," declared Reid, before Leslie could commit herself. "Leslie has had too much worry lately. I want to give her a little happiness and gaiety."

"In Paris?" Caroline's glance slid over him with a degree of significance which Leslie curiously resented.

"We might spend part of our honeymoon in Paris," Reid agreed. "What do you say?" And he smiled an indulgent query at Leslie.

"That would be — lovely. I've never been to Paris."

"You'll enjoy showing Paris to someone who's never seen it, won't you?" Caroline said.

Then she apparently saw an acquaintance the other side of the room, and she nodded carelessly to Reid and Leslie and moved away.

For almost a minute after she had gone there was silence between them. Then Reid said softly and amusedly,

"The value of shock tactics."

"Do you think they — worked?"

"At least we arrested her attention."

"Oh, certainly."

Reid glanced at her sharply.

"Weren't you satisfied with our degree of success?"

"I don't know——" Leslie moved uneasily. "You know her better than I do. But I thought it was more a question of — of pique, than horrified realization of a mistake on her own part."

He frowned impatiently.

"One doesn't expect to reverse the whole position at one blow."

"No, of course not. Only——"

"Yes?"

"Oh, sometimes it seems to me that we just plunge deeper and deeper into a very doubtful situation, without achieving much of what we hope to do."

He grinned, however, at that.

"You're not a natural gambler, darling," he said,

90

patting her hand as it lay on the table. "I know what shook you. The talk of a Paris honeymoon, wasn't it?"

She flushed and laughed reluctantly.

"No — not really. Except that it seemed to make everything alarmingly real and detailed all at once. But it's all right. I was just being silly, I expect." Then she glanced at him curiously and said, "You both know Paris very well, don't you?"

"As far as two people in love ever know a place which is simply a background to their happiness."

She gave him a smile of warm sympathy and exclaimed impulsively, "Oh, I hope you get her, if you really want her so much!"

"Definitely withdrawn your backing from Oliver, eh?" he asked teasingly.

"Oh — Oliver——" She had forgotten about him for the last half-hour. "I wasn't backing Oliver anyway, as you most vulgarly put it. Surely I've done enough to show I don't want him to marry Caroline!"

"Yes, yes. I was really thinking of how eagerly you canvassed dear Oliver's happiness, as being the most important thing in all this."

"I still think his happiness most important," she countered a little resentfully.

"Fine," he said rather dryly. And then they rose to go.

She thought how amazing his self-control was, that he even managed to leave the place without so much as a backward glance at where Caroline was sitting. If it had been Oliver who was sitting there, could she have done as much? She thought not.

At home once more, she received the fresh congratulations and comments of her family on her beautiful engagement ring, and contrived to look happy and carefree, even when Alma put her own thoughts into words with a reflective, "It seems to make it much more *real,* when you wear a ring."

Leslie turned away quickly and said, "Did you tell Morley, Mother?"

"Oh, yes, dear. He said he thought he'd seen something like that coming."

She laughed incredulously and with a good deal of relief.

"He said *that?* In what tone exactly?"

"How do you mean?"

"Well, was he pleased, dissatisfied, sceptical, shocked — what?"

Her mother laughed in her turn.

"I couldn't say, my dear. You'll have to find that out yourself."

"Can I go and see him now?"

"No. I think I'd leave him to rest, if I were you. He was a good deal exhausted by the examination and is probably sleeping now."

"Of course."

"But if you want to do something, I wish you'd pop over to Dr. Bendick's surgery, Leslie, and get his medicine."

"Why, yes. I'll go at once."

Not at all displeased to escape on her own and have a respite from playing her rather exacting role, Leslie slipped on a coat and went out by the side gate. It was a pleasant walk to the Bendicks' house, and if she only knocked at the surgery entrance she could probably escape seeing either the doctor or his wife, and avoid any further comment or question. Oliver, she was sure, would have returned to his job by now.

But in this she had miscalculated. Leslie had only just received the medicine at the hands of the surgery assistant and turned away to take the path home through the woods, when Oliver's voice hailed her, urgently — even a little peremptorily — and he came quickly along the garden path to overtake her.

"Hello. I thought you'd gone back."

"No. I've some extra time. But what's this extraordinary story Father's got hold of?"

"About Morley?"

"No. About you." He fell into step beside her, with

92

a purposeful air which said that he was accompanying her until he had found out all he wanted to.

She felt her heart flutter dangerously and her breath come a little unevenly, but she managed to say quite calmly,

"Oh, you mean my engagement. I know it's very sudden, but it's quite true. I'm engaged to Reid."

"But you can't be! I never heard of such nonsense. You've not known the fellow a week. And, anyway, he's simply not your sort."

"Oliver dear, are you so sure you know what 'my sort' is?"

"Of course I do. I've known you all your life, haven't I?"

"And never guessed the most important thing about me," thought Leslie, with faintly bitter amusement.

Aloud she said, "I don't know that that helps much. I was just a bit surprised that Caroline appealed to you quite so powerfully. I don't think even the best of friends are very good at guessing things about each other when it comes to falling in love."

"But, Leslie——" He was evidently deeply disturbed, and she thought how much she loved him for it. "I don't think you even know this Reid well enough to have made up your mind properly. You're usually so well-balanced, so — so sane and unhurried. This whole business isn't a bit like you."

She laughed — without much effort, because it made her feel light-hearted, and just a little light-headed too, to have Oliver worrying about her in this way.

"But, Oliver, you can't expect anyone to be well-balanced and sane over falling in love. It's a contradiction in terms, surely?"

He looked at her gloomily and said,

"You really are in love with him, then?"

"Why, of course. You don't think I would — would marry for any other reason, do you?"

"Yes. That was the very thing I was afraid of," he assured her with some grimness. "I thought you were marrying him because he'd inherited all your great-aunt's money, and you didn't see how the hell the family was going to manage if you didn't do something about it."

"I suppose it's bound to look a bit like that," she conceded, with a judicial air which she privately thought rather good. "But that isn't what decided me, Oliver. Really and truly it isn't."

"You're asking me to believe that you've fallen so hopelessly and romantically in love with this comparative stranger that, in the course of a couple of days, you're quite sure you want to spend the rest of your life with him? Leslie, do think again. I'm sure you're making the most dreadful mistake."

"What you mean is that you don't like him," Leslie retorted, and because she did like Reid, the faint hostility in her voice was genuine.

"I can't stand him," agreed Oliver with great heartiness. "I think he's self-confident to a degree, and cynical and arrogant too. And I think you're being silly and wilfully blind, just because he's good-looking and rich and excessively male."

"Oliver!"

There was an astonished silence. Then he said, in a slightly shamed tone,

"I'm sorry I called you silly."

"Oh, it's not *that.*" She brushed the mild insult aside. "Do you really see Reid like that?" she asked curiously.

"More or less."

"You're quite wrong, you know." Suddenly she found herself most anxious to justify Reid to Oliver. "He isn't a bit like that."

"Not self-confident?" he queried dryly.

"Well——" She laughed.

"Or arrogant, or cynical? My dear Leslie, use your excellent judgment!"

"It's a very good-natured cynicism, Oliver. I rather like it."

"You *rather like it?* Good God, girl," exclaimed Oliver, who had never addressed her like that in her life before, "do you realize you're talking about the qualities of the man you say you love? One doesn't 'rather like' things about the person one proposes to marry."

"Do you more than rather like the way Caroline looks at other men?" she asked suddenly, and then was astonished that she could speak so coolly and ironically to Oliver.

"Caroline doesn't enter into this," he said stiffly, after another astonished little silence.

"Oh, yes, she does! Believe me, I'm quite as much surprised at your choice as you are at mine," exclaimed Leslie, suddenly feeling some wise precaution in her collapse, so that she had a horrid feeling that she was going to say things for which she would be sorry, while being powerless to stop herself. "If anyone had told me beforehand that Caroline was the kind of girl to attract you, I'd have said 'Nonsense' in my turn. But it's your own business. I'm not trying to dissuade you from marrying her, am I? I've given you my congratulations and decided to mind my own business. Even if you decide afterwards that you made a mistake and don't want her after all, I'm not going to say 'I could have told you.' It's for you——"

"I should hope not, indeed!" He was nearly as indignant as she by now. "And what on earth should give you the idea that I might change my mind about Caroline? I never heard of anything so ridiculous, and I very much resent it."

Aloud she said, making a great effort to speak calmly,

"I'm sorry, Oliver. It wasn't very tasteful of me to use your own circumstances to reinforce my argument. But we're both being rather angry and ill-balanced about this. Don't you think we ought to agree not to interfere with each other?"

"Leslie——" He took her arm, and he too had lost his anger now. "I don't mean to interfere, my dear. But you mean a great deal to me — you're like my own family——"

"I know. Like a sister," she said, and somehow she kept the irony out of her voice that time.

"Well — something like that. I can't help knowing that neither of your parents would give you much good advice over this. Your father will see only the material advantages, particularly to himself, and your mother, bless her, will be swayed this way and that by her sentiment and her desire to think the best of everything. Morley's in no condition to take a hand. I *can't* let you do this thing without protesting. There was a time when you'd have conceded my right to do so. I seem to have lost touch with you, Leslie, and I don't know whether I am to blame myself or not."

"You're not to blame in any way," she assured him quickly. "And I don't really mind your talking to me, Oliver dear. Only I can't have you speaking against Reid. You must see I can't."

He was silent for a moment. Then he said in a more reasonable tone,

"Well, you won't rush into a hasty marriage, will you?"

She thought of what Reid had said to Caroline that very afternoon.

"We haven't made any definite decision yet." That much she had to concede him. "But no one has a very long engagement nowadays. I don't expect you mean to yourself, do you?"

He looked faintly restive once more at being side-tracked on to his own affairs.

"We haven't decided either," he said rather curtly.

"Well, then, couldn't we both agree to leave our affairs in a pleasant state of uncertainty for the moment?" They had reached the side gate of Cranley Magna by now and she turned, smiling, to face him. "Are you coming in?"

"Not tonight. I expect you're right about leaving our affairs uncertain for the moment. At any rate, your affairs."

"Oh, no, Oliver!" She laughed. "I didn't mean it

in that sense. What I meant was that neither of us seems likely to rush into an irrevocable decision in the next twenty-four hours, so let's agree not to question each other closely." She held out her hand in a friendly way, but with an air of decision.

He took her hand a little doubtfully, as though he still hardly knew what to make of her in this new mood.

"No hard feelings about my interference?" he said, with a wry smile.

"None at all, Oliver. I'm a good deal — touched that you should care enough about me to feel so anxious."

"Good lord, Leslie! You know how much I — well, anyway, I wouldn't have any unhappiness come to any one of you girls if I could prevent it."

"I know you wouldn't." Her tone was still friendly, but a shade colder that time. And she withdrew her hand with a definite "Good night."

But as she turned away he detained her a moment longer.

"Leslie——"

"Yes?" She turned back, a little surprised.

"What did you mean, exactly, when you spoke of the — the way Caroline looks at other men?"

She experienced a disagreeable little shock. Perhaps at being pinned down to her own unwise wording. Perhaps at the discovery that his final thoughts ran, after all, on Caroline.

"I — nothing very much. I spoke hastily."

"But you must have been thinking of something definite when you said that." He looked obstinate and, she thought, vaguely disturbed.

"I'm sorry. I suppose it was a rather — catty remark. It would be nicer — and just as true — to say that she has very beautiful eyes and knows how to use them to advantage. I didn't want to imply any more than that."

He smiled, not entirely satisfied, she saw. Then he said,

"She can't help attracting people, of course." And, with a friendly wave of his hand, he left her.

As she crossed the lawn, Reid came out of one of the french windows to meet her.

"Was that Oliver who escorted you home?"

"It was."

He glanced at her, evidently speculating on the reason for her curtness.

"Had he anything to say about your engagement?"

"Good gracious, yes! A lecture under three headings. His anxiety, my foolishness and your undesirability."

Reid laughed and began to look as though he were enjoying himself.

"Do tell me what he said about me?"

"No. Your ego is quite sufficiently developed as it is."

"Don't tell me he praised me?"

"Of course not. But to a man of your type, some censure is better than praise."

"That's true," he agreed equably. "I won't question you about the particular, then. I'll just ask, in general terms, did he react as you hoped he would?"

"Oh, Reid——" She pushed back her hair with sudden weariness. "I don't know. Sometimes I ask myself what I'm really trying to do. If it weren't too late to turn back, I'd say it's wrong and ridiculous to interfere so arrogantly with the natural course of events."

"There is no natural course of events, my sweet," he told her, smiling, but rather kindly. "There are those who direct events and those who submit to them. You are in the habit of submitting, and it worries you to find yourself moving the pieces on the board, instead of being moved around. But you're tired——" He put his arm round her lightly and, somehow, rather comfortingly. "Don't torment yourself with any more self-analysis. Be satisfied if your Oliver showed signs of being concerned about your welfare and anxious about your future. Stop planning, and let events take their course during the next few days. We have done all the interfering that's necessary for the moment."

"Thank heaven for that," Leslie retorted grimly.

But he laughed, and lightly kissed the side of her cheek. And for no reason that she could possibly define, she felt her spirits rise once more.

During the next few days, to her immeasurable relief, it really did seem that events might be permitted to take their own course. Reid and she had established the idea of their engagement, not only in the minds of the family, but also with Caroline and Oliver. It remained now to be seen what gradual reaction this would provoke.

Twice Caroline telephoned, and each time she unashamedly asked for Reid. He didn't offer to give Leslie his version of the conversations. But she heard snatches of the first one, and again she had the impression of two people who knew each other remarkably well sparring gaily and feeling out each other's defences.

One afternoon Leslie had the opportunity of a long, quiet talk with her brother. He had kept to his own room since the specialist's visit and now was only waiting for a vacancy in Sir James Trevant's nursing home. Leslie found him in a curiously tranquil, indulgent sort of mood, luxuriating in freedom from the secret anxiety about his health which, she realized now, must have weighed terribly on his spirits in recent months.

"You feel every confidence in Sir James, don't you, Morley?" she said to him, noticing with delight the brightness of his eyes and the hopeful lift to the corners of his mouth.

"Yes. I have no doubt at all that he can make me better. And if I believed that any man could make me walk again, I should believe it of Trevant."

"Do you mean," Leslie said almost fearfully, "that you think there *might* be a chance of his doing that?"

"I don't know." Morley idly curled the tassel of

his dressing-gown round his hand. "I only know that *he* thinks there's a chance."

"Did he say so?"

"No. But he has the most expressive face I've ever seen. And I know he thinks there's a faint chance. So faint that he couldn't possibly mention it to me. But that's one reason why he's so anxious to have me in his nursing-home, under his own eye."

"Morley! I — I hardly dare even think of such a thing."

"Nor I. But the thought of it made the taking of Reid's money more justified, somehow."

"Oh, Morley, you don't have to think of that! Reid told me, with all sincerity, that he would give every penny of Great-Aunt Tabitha's money if it would make you well."

"Because he's in love with you?"

"Oh, n—— Well, yes. I suppose so."

"And you took him on those terms?"

"No, Morley. That isn't true."

"Are you telling me that you love him?"

She hesitated only a second before she said, "Certainly."

"Swear it?" He was smiling at her, but his eyes were bright and exceedingly watchful.

She passed the tip of her tongue over her lips.

"I swear that I'm not marrying Reid for his money."

Morley gave her a long, thoughtful look.

"You changed that wording, didn't you?" he said musingly. "I wonder why. You wouldn't swear that you love him."

"Please, Morley, don't go imagining things. Believe me, I had agreed to become engaged to Reid *before* I knew about your needing this expensive treatment."

"Because of the family?"

"No. Because of myself."

He laughed, not altogether satisfied, she saw. But he was too happy and hopeful about his own prospects to question her more closely. Besides, Morley being Morley, he would undoubtedly concede that she had a right to reticence about her own affairs. Having satisfied himself that no specific sacrifice had been made on his behalf, he obviously considered that anything further was, broadly speaking, her own business.

To Leslie's delight and relief, when the summons finally came for Morley to go to the nursing-home, she was the one who was chosen to accompany him and see him safely installed. Reid offered to accompany them too. But Morley was not enthusiastic and, since Dr. Bendick insisted on being of the party, Reid's presence was not really necessary.

For two or three days, Leslie stayed on in London, although Dr. Bendick, having seen his patient safely installed, returned to Cranleymere the same day. She rather enjoyed the curiously detached existence of one stranger among many other strangers in a quiet hotel, and it was wonderful not to have to pretend about herself to anyone. Each day she went to see Morley, so that in those first difficult days he should not feel bereft of everything and everyone familiar. But towards the end of the week he said to her,

"If you want to get back to the family — and Reid — you don't need to hang about here any longer on my behalf, you know."

"I'm rather enjoying it, as a matter of fact." Leslie smiled.

"You are? Curious point of view for a newly engaged girl," Morley remarked, with his characteristically quizzical glance.

"Well——" She coloured a little. "I meant, really, that anyone can enjoy herself in London for a few days, and I don't want to go until you feel perfectly settled here."

"I am perfectly settled, my dear. And though I enjoy seeing you every afternoon, that can hardly go on indefinitely and may as well stop now as any other time. Besides" — he smiled with that touch of real sweetness which could sometimes irradiate his thin, sardonic young face — "I owe Reid enough. It's not exactly fair to keep you away from him too."

"Oh——" She looked faintly surprised, because she never could quite get used to the idea that Reid was supposed to be consumed with passion for her. "I dare say—— Well, perhaps you're right, Morley."

"I think I probably am," he agreed. And they arranged then that Leslie should return within the next two days, though probably she, or another of the family, would visit him again in a few weeks' time.

As she made her preparations for returning home, Leslie found her thoughts running on ahead of her. To everyone expecting a letter — some news — an event, it always seems that a short absence from home works some sort of miracle. Because one has not been there to watch every post and every change of event, it seems that limitless opportunities must have occurred for the thing one hoped or dreaded to have happened.

As the train drew slowly and reluctantly into the station, she caught a glimpse of Reid's car standing outside.

Well — it had been rather fantastic to imagine that Oliver might somehow be there. Reid was perhaps the one best suited to give her the news. And as she came out of the station and he got out of the car to open the door for her, she greeted him with a brilliant smile.

"Everything satisfactory so far as Morley is concerned, I see," he observed. And she laughed and agreed that this was so.

While they drove down the slope from the station and along the first half-mile of the road home, she gave him further details about her brother, and the one or two items of personal news about her stay in London. But when they turned into the long, familiar, winding lane which eventually led to Cranley Magna, he slowed the car and, as though sensing that something was coming, she said,

"You didn't write to me, Reid."

"No. Did you expect me to?"

"Only if there were — something special to tell me."

102

"There was nothing special to tell you, during the first five days."

She was indescribably chilled and disappointed.

"You mean — nothing at all happened?"

"Nothing."

"No — news of either Oliver or Caroline?"

"Not until yesterday."

"And then there was some news?"

"Yes."

"Of which of them?"

"Of both."

"Well, then, tell me," she cried, half frightened suddenly by his manner, though she hardly knew why. "What happened?"

"They were married, Leslie, by special licence, yesterday morning."

CHAPTER EIGHT

THERE was complete and stunned silence for perhaps twenty seconds, except for the sound of the motor. Then Leslie cried,

"I don't believe it! It can't possibly be true. I simply don't believe it. Is this some ridiculous sort of joke or something?"

"It is not a joke," Reid said flatly. "It's the simple, damnable, inescapable truth. Oliver and Caroline are now man and wife, and so far as we and our schemes are concerned, we can call it a day."

Even in that moment she resented the word "schemes," but these silly details had no significance any more. She stared at him helplessly, wondering why she had not noticed before that he looked grim and strained.

At last she said, "How did it happen?" Heavily, like one enquiring for details of a fatal accident.

"I don't know."

"Well then, how did you hear about it?"

"Mrs. Bendick telephoned your mother and told her. I gather she and the Doctor were a bit upset. But why they did it, or what decided them to act so suddenly, I don't know. And I've been such a complete fool in all my calculations up to now that I'd rather someone else made the next guess."

She was silent again, delving reluctantly into the recesses of her memory. Had there been anything — anything at all — in her conversation with Oliver which could have given her the slightest hint of what was coming?

"He said" — she was speaking her thoughts aloud — "that they hadn't come to any decision about the length of their engagement. Oliver *said* that to me, not two weeks ago."

"Well, they came to a decision," retorted Reid dryly. "A pretty thorough one, it seems."

"But there was nothing——"

She stopped suddenly, and passed her hand over her eyes.

"Oh — wait a minute! I said something stupid——"

"*You* did?"

"Yes. About — about the way Caroline looked at other men. She — has a special way, you know."

"You're telling me," he said dryly, and Leslie muttered,

"Oh, I'm sorry."

"Never mind. Go on. What did he say then?"

"At the time he was just angry, and I more or less took the words back. Then we got off the subject. But, just as we were separating — when we'd been talking of quite other things, I mean, and come to a more or less agreeable understanding — he said, as a sort of afterthought, 'What did you mean exactly, when you spoke of the way Caroline looks at other men?'"

"I thought I got out of it fairly neatly, Reid. I thought I satisfied him. But I think I know now why he was so angry with me. It was not that he felt I did her an injustice. It was that what I said made him really jealous."

"So what?" He stared ahead gloomily at an awkward corner.

"Why, don't you see? Sooner or later that induced him to have some sort of showdown with her about her — her attracting other men. I suppose she protested that it all meant nothing. And to prove it — or perhaps just to seal their reconciliation after they had had a row about it — she suggested they should get married right away. It was the perfect answer to the suspicions that *I* had been fool enough to put into his mind. And Oliver would be swept off his feet by such a gesture, you know. He would fall for it unhesitatingly. In fact, I probably had quite a lot to do with hurrying on the one thing we hoped to delay," she finished bitterly.

He considered that in silence. Then he took his

hand from the wheel and patted hers, rather as he had the first time they met. A familiarity which, she remembered, had annoyed her greatly at that time.

"I don't think I'd torment myself with that one, if I were you," he said. And the touch, as well as the words, oddly comforted her.

"I shall always feel I muffed my part, though," she said with a sigh. "And after you had shown such skill in managing her too."

"Like hell I did!" He laughed rather bitterly in his turn. "I flattered myself I was such a smart fellow, rousing healthy doubt and jealousy in her. Don't you remember, you told me at the time that you thought she wasn't suffering from anything more than pique? Quite right, my dear! And what I was suffering from was wilful blindness and egregious conceit."

"Oh, no, Reid!" She thought he was being a little too hard on himself.

"Um-hm. I just couldn't, or wouldn't, accept the fact that she might prefer someone else to me."

"It is rather difficult to accept these things," Leslie said sadly. "Poor Reid! I'm so sorry. In a way, it's much worse for you."

"Hell! Why?" he wanted to know.

"Because you hadn't ever really imagined losing. I'd already had my major shock. *I* could never quite imagine our hopes succeeding."

He laughed reluctantly.

"Sweetheart, I'm most dreadfully sorry too," he said ruefully. "I'm entirely responsible for waking all sorts of hopes in you which your courage and determination were trying to put to sleep. I wonder if I haven't let you down even worse than Oliver."

"Oh, no, Reid!" Again she felt she could not have him blame himself so completely. "I was just as anxious as you to try what we could do. Well, nearly," she amended. At which he laughed again and said,

"The proportion of blame doesn't much matter now, I guess. Look — we're in sight of Cranley Magna.

106

Do you feel able to face them? Or do you want me to drive around a bit?"

"Oh, no! I'll face them," she exclaimed, with a touch of obstinate pride. "I've learned a little about self-control in the last few weeks and, anyway, I'd be ashamed not to be able to — to hide anything like that from the family. Besides, they will be longing to hear every detail about Morley, you know. It wouldn't be fair to keep them waiting."

"Good girl," he said approvingly, and turned in at the gates of Cranley Magna.

It was not so difficult, really, Leslie thought, when they all crowded round her in the drawing-room later, eager for the latest news of Morley. They wanted to know how he had looked, if she had left him cheerful, what she thought of the nursing-home, and any possible information she might have gleaned about Sir James Trevant himself and his hopes of success.

They were so affectionate to her and, through her, to Morley that, if she concentrated hard on what they were saying and on what they wanted to know, she could almost ignore that great aching blank which had replaced all her hopes and fears and expectations so far as Oliver was concerned.

Until half-way through tea they continued their questions, and she her account of her stay in London. Then at last Alma, who had obviously been bursting with ill-suppressed news on her side for the last few minutes, said,

"You'll never guess what *we* have to tell *you*."

"Sorry, Alma. I'm afraid I told Leslie," Reid put in contritely. "Did I steal your scoop?"

"Well" — Alma looked a little dashed — "I didn't think of your being interested enough to tell her. After all, you hardly knew Oliver, did you?"

"True," Reid agreed. "But I did," he added dryly, "know Caroline."

"Yes, of course. I'd forgotten that. But it wasn't as though she *meant* anything much to you," Alma explained comfortably. "Oliver was about our oldest friend."

"Yes, since you put it that way, I do see it must have been a shock to you."

Alma looked surprised.

"Well, I don't know about a shock," she said protestingly. "After all, a marriage is something nice, isn't it?"

"That," Reid assured her, "depends entirely on the parties concerned — and the circumstances."

Richard Greeve gave his mellow, understanding man-to-man laugh.

"All right, my dear boy. No one expects you to take much interest in any marriage but your own at this point. And indeed all of us — now that we have such excellent reports of our dear Morley — can prepare with confidence and pleasure for what I might call that next event in the family's affairs."

For a moment Leslie looked so blank that Reid gave her a warning glance. And, with reluctance, her mind accepted the idea that, to the outside observer, nothing in their affairs had changed. Though Oliver and Caroline might have rendered their engagement a tragic farce from the point of view of Reid and herself, in the eyes of the family she and Reid were as firmly and happily linked as ever. Not only that. The family's comfortable enjoyment in the good news about Morley depended for what one might call its financial support on that engagement continuing.

All at once she felt indescribably trapped. She wanted to cry out against the forces which were being gently and smilingly arrayed around her. But, even as the idea came to her, she heard Reid, calmly and pleasantly, answering some specific enquiry which her father had added to his genial, if heavy, generalization.

"We didn't think of making any very definite arrangements until Morley was home again, sir," he was saying, aware — as Leslie knew — that an occasional "sir" tended to put Richard Greeve in an excellent humour.

On this occasion, however, he was more intent on seeing that no one departed from a line of conduct which should have the desirable result of providing financial stability without imposing any slight on his personal pride.

"We don't need to let the affairs of one member of the family wait so exactly on those of another," he stated agreeably but firmly. "There is no reason whatever, my dear Reid, for you and Leslie to wait for your happiness. Indeed, though I deprecate any such unseemly haste as Oliver has shown, nothing would please me — or my family," he added as an inconsiderable afterthought, "more than to have you and Leslie fix an early date for your wedding. For my part, I was going to suggest——"

"Oh, Father, do leave us to settle these things for ourselves!" exclaimed Leslie, her nerves drawn taut, so that she spoke with unusual irritation.

All she had done by her impatient objection, she saw now, was to fix her father's attention, with offended determination, on the whole question of an early marriage.

"I keep on making mistakes in technique, it seems," she said ruefully to Reid later, when they snatched a few moments alone together. "It makes me feel afraid to open my mouth."

He laughed and patted her shoulder consolingly.

"Your father will forget about wedding arrangements in some new interest quite soon."

"Oh, no." Leslie shook her head. "You don't know him, Reid, if you can say that. He's got his teeth into this business now, and just won't let go. Besides——" She stopped, coloured a little and looked distressed.

"All right. Don't distress yourself about it. I know quite well that there's the money aspect. The poor old boy feels — not unjustifiably — that he'll be a lot more comfortable when he has a rich daughter than when he merely has a rich prospective son-in-law."

Leslie thought how greatly her father would have resented being referred to as a poor old boy. But the statement, as such, represented the situation exactly.

"I know it must seem hypocritical and inconsistent of him," she said apologetically, "to strike such an attitude of pride and integrity about refusing to take money from a stranger, and then to try, with almost indecent haste, to hustle that stranger into becoming a relation, so that he can profit from the arrangement with almost ingenuous openness. But, Reid, he honestly believes in the essential rightness of both attitudes. Both the pride, I mean, and the genial plundering of a close relation."

"Yes. I've worked that out some time ago," Reid assured her good-humouredly. "And as, in my heart, I consider the money largely his by right, I don't very much mind by what specious argument he can convince himself that he may take it. What does worry me is that, so far, he seems only willing to accept it if it's offered, so to speak, on our marriage certificate."

"Reid, I don't know how you can joke about it! It's terribly serious, you know."

"Terribly," agreed Reid, with a grin. "I feel the bands of matrimony tighten round me every time he calls me 'my dear boy.'"

She laughed reluctantly. And then, because she had been through enough to test the strongest nerves, she suddenly felt the tears come.

"I wish — I knew — what to do." She had turned away from him, but the unevenness of her voice betrayed her.

"Sweetheart, don't cry." He came up behind her.

"I'm not crying."

"Well, don't sound so exactly as though you are, then," he said, and took her in his arms.

"Oh, *Reid!*" She turned against him, and found the strangest comfort in being held very tightly while she sobbed once or twice.

"Now look, honey, nothing's ever so bad that one can't make something of it." He ruffled her hair, with a half-amused, half-tender gesture. "You've had altogether too much to handle lately. But, although I made such a howling fiasco of the Caroline-Oliver business, I promise you I'll get you out of this somehow."

"Oh, it isn't really that. At least, of course, it is partly. Only everything seems so — so out of hand and I can't see my way ahead one little bit, and—— Well, anyway, that's how it is."

"I know. And, most of all, the thing you didn't mention. It must be the very devil losing your confounded Oliver all over again."

She was silent. Then she nodded her head slightly, because he seemed to expect her to. But to her immense surprise she realized that, until he mentioned Oliver, she hadn't really been thinking of him.

"We can't do anything for the moment but go on with this engagement. You do see that, don't you?"

"Yes, of course." She wasn't really paying much attention to him. She was turning over in her mind the incredible fact that "losing Oliver all over again," as Reid put it, was not the agonizing central point of her distress, as it should have been.

"He has *really* gone this time. He's Caroline's husband," she told herself, like someone pressing on a doubtful tooth to see if it really ached.

But there was a sort of dull acceptance, rather than anguished protest, and she told herself that she was probably past feeling very acutely about anything that day.

"Feeling better?" enquired Reid at that moment. And she laughed, because she knew there was no reason why she should be feeling better, except for his comforting presence. Only she did.

"Much better," she said, and flung her arms round him, as she had that time in the hall when she had first known that she could call on every penny he had to make Morley well. "Much, much better, Reid. Because one can't help feeling better and more hope-

111

ful when you're around. There's something about you. It's your — your special gift to mankind."

"Make it womankind," he said, and kissed her. Not just a light, teasing kiss. But the kiss of someone who had shared some varied experiences with her and valued her after the test. She felt the rather hard line of his cheek against hers, and knew the most real and primitive consolation of all — the sheer physical contact of someone in whom there was the answering spark of understanding.

It became clear during the next few days, however, that no one else in the family was thinking of her engagement in terms of prolonging it. Only from the point of view of shortening it.

Even Alma said importantly,

"I'll have to know fairly soon about the wedding, because I suppose I'll be a bridesmaid, and it'll mean getting a day's holiday from school."

"Maybe we shan't have the wedding until your next holidays," Leslie said, with seeming carelessness.

"Oh, Leslie! You *couldn't* delay it as long as that! Besides, I think it's mean of you to talk about having it in the holidays. What a *waste* of a perfectly good reason for having a day off."

Alma looked so reproachful that Leslie had to laugh and say that at least she would keep that important point in mind.

"Anyway, what's the need for delay?" Alma threw at her as a parting shot, as she flounced off into the garden on some affairs of her own.

"Yes, Leslie dear. What need *is* there for delay?" asked her mother, the only other person who had been in the room when this conversation took place.

"There isn't any, Mother!" Leslie tried to look perfectly natural and mildly surprised at the question. "Some people like a longer engagement than others."

"But I thought—— The whole impression in the beginning was that you were both swept off your feet, and the sooner you were married the happier you would both be."

"Well, of — of course. But there's no *frantic* hurry. It's just that Father has this bee in his bonnet about it."

"No, darling, it isn't. No one wants to hurry you. Not even your Father really." This was said without complete conviction. "Only, there's no denying that, if you are both sure of your own minds, in the — the peculiar circumstances, an early marriage would certainly solve a lot of difficulties. As it is——" She broke off and sighed.

"You mean that the day-to-day financial position is pretty grim?"

"I'm afraid so. I hate to sound as though we're only waiting to sponge on Reid, but——"

"It isn't sponging! Reid told me himself that he regards Great-Aunt Tabitha's money as largely Father's own due."

"I know, Leslie dear. He told us that too, and I'm quite sure he means it. But you know what your Father is. He keeps on saying that he wants the position regularized."

"Well!" cried Leslie in amused indignation. "I can think of better ways of describing my wedding."

Her mother smiled too. But passingly, like someone whose worries were too near for her to indulge in real laughter.

"He means, you know, that once the family is one, so to speak, there is a perfectly just basis for discussing how the money should be divided. Until then, he says he feels he can't accept any of the money without putting himself in the undignified position of a man who 'touches' his prospective son-in-law for a loan, on the strength of doubtful expectations."

Leslie inwardly cursed her father's preposterous hair-splitting, which dictated stubborn pride in one set of circumstances and almost ingenuous exploitation in another.

"I know, darling. I do understand." She glanced affectionately at her mother, and wished anxiously that she looked less harassed. It made one feel so horribly guilty.

113

"I wouldn't have spoken like this, Leslie — it's so entirely your own business, dear, I do know that — only" — for a moment her mother smiled almost brilliantly — "I feel so reassured by the way you look at Reid sometimes."

Leslie was astounded.

"The way I look at Reid?" she repeated. "How do I look at him?"

"Oh, I was thinking of the way your face lights up when he comes into the room, as though you feel that, the moment he appears, any worries are over."

"Oh — oh, yes. Of course."

"And then sometimes you have such a sweet look of — discovery, darling." Her mother's smile became very affectionate. "As though you hardly know yourself how fond you are of him. Lots of engaged girls become very gay and confident in their attitude, you know. You aren't a bit like that. It's as though you feel you're trembling on the verge of a still greater discovery any moment."

"Mother, you — you're fanciful." Leslie had gone very pale suddenly.

"Oh, Leslie dear, you mustn't mind my noticing these things. Mothers do like to flatter themselves that they have a very special understanding about their daughters. At least, sentimental mothers do. And I suppose I'm sentimental," Mrs. Greeve said, without regret.

"You certainly are." Leslie laughed, trying to make the laugh sound indulgent and understanding.

But it came out rather shaky and uncertain.

"Do I — really — look at Reid like that?"

"Occasionally, in the last few days. You needn't be so taken aback, dear." Her mother was genuinely amused. "It's quite a proper way for an engaged girl to look."

"Yes — I know. I only thought——"

Her voice trailed off into dismayed silence. But as her father's voice was heard in the hall just then demanding to know where his wife was, Leslie's silence passed unremarked. In fact, Mrs. Greeve got up and hurried out to her husband, and Leslie was left alone in the room.

Slowly she went to the mirror over the fireplace and studied her own pale reflection.

Stupid of her to have lost her colour like that. She hoped her mother had not noticed. But even now her eyes widened and darkened again as she thought of the words which had given her such a shock. A shock of half-acknowledged realization.

"It's as though you feel you're trembling on the verge of a still greater discovery any moment," was what her mother had said. And her mother was a singularly acute woman where people were concerned.

"It couldn't be true! Oh, Reid, it couldn't possibly be true!"

Leslie dropped her head on her arms on the mantelpiece, and tried to recall her horror and heartbreak when she had first known that Oliver was lost to her. In that moment, she would almost have welcomed a return of the first anguish she had suffered that evening in the wood. But she felt — she admitted it ruthlessly — a sort of nostalgic regret. Nothing more.

"But perhaps I am just getting over him — quite naturally. It doesn't *have* to be a case of one passion driving out another. Mother is just being fanciful. And so — am I." She raised her head and looked at herself for a long time again. "Or am I?" she said aloud at last.

"Are you what, my sweet?"

He had come into the room without her noticing, but at the sound of his voice she swung round to face him, colouring, so that no one could have guessed how pale she had been only a few minutes ago.

"Oh, I——" She laughed embarrassingly. "It's a bad habit, talking to one's own reflection. I think I was just asking myself if I — if I were really managing the present situation well," she finished hastily.

"So far as a masterly inactivity can be described as

doing things well, we are managing splendidly," he assured her. "But it's no good concealing the fact from ourselves — we are merely marking time. There *will* be a moment when we simply have to make a decision. And, so far as I can see, we're neither of us one whit nearer knowing what that decision will be."

"If we could only make Father see things in a more sensible light——" Leslie sighed. But, even as she said the words, she knew they were a waste of time and breath. Her father had taken up a particularly obstinate line on the question of the inheritance, and — as an extension of the same question — her marriage. Nothing would move him now.

And as though echoing her thoughts, Reid said regretfully,

"It's damned difficult to un-strike an attitude. Your father couldn't do it without a considerable sacrifice of pride. Can you see him climbing down? Because I can't."

"No, no. Of course he wouldn't do that. I know once or twice in the past he's made things dreadfully difficult by taking up a stand that he couldn't abandon without looking silly. Nothing would change him now. I do believe he would literally rather starve, or — or even sacrifice Morley's best interests. But then — what can we *do?*"

Reid gave her a rather quizzical glance. Then, with his hands in his pockets, he strolled slowly up the room and back again.

"There are two courses open to us, my pet. There always have been. We can either tell the exact truth and have your father order me from the house, refuse all financial help and generally plunge you into disaster while I return to France or——"

"Oh, Reid!"

At the thought of his going she was assailed by such cold despair that she felt literally sick.

"Or," he said reflectively, "we could, quite simply, go on with this marriage."

"You — you mean in actual fact?"

"I mean in actual fact."

"But——" She turned away from him, in case he should see from her face that, for her, the heavens had suddenly opened and the angels sung. "But — you said — there would never be any girl but Caroline for you."

"Sure." The angels stopped singing, and the world went grey again. "Sure. And you said there would never be any man but Oliver for you. We were both right, of course. But the question is — what does any sensible person do when he can't have the thing he has set his heart on?"

"He — he makes do with the second best," she stammered, fascinated into saying what she supposed he wanted her to say.

"It sounds a bit ungracious, put into words," he said with a laugh. "But it applies to both of us equally. We know an awful lot about each other, honey, so that we don't have to pretend the least little bit. Look here——" He turned again and came towards her.

"Don't take me in your arms!" she thought wildly. "Don't take me in your arms, or I shall give myself away."

But he didn't put his arms round her. He took both her hands lightly in his.

"It's like this. We've both lost out on the thing that means most in the world to us, but we have a good deal in common, Leslie, besides that experience. After a rather bad start, I think we've always liked — possibly admired — each other. I know I admire most things about you. I can give you a pretty good married life, and I can make your family happy and free from anxiety. It's not a bad basis, my dear."

She stared at him wordlessly. And after a moment he said,

"There's no need to hurry. Think it over. But, if you marry me, I promise that most of your problems will be over. If you don't — God knows when or how they can be solved."

"I know," she said almost in a whisper. "I know — that's true."

But she was not really thinking about that. At least, not much.

She was thinking of her mother saying that she sometimes looked as though she were trembling on the verge of a great discovery. She had made that discovery now.

It was Reid she loved. The long pretence had become a reality. But only with her. Not with him.

CHAPTER NINE

LESLIE wondered afterwards how long she stood there, with her hands slack in Reid's, while she tried to make up her mind on the most momentous question of her life.

If she married him, she knew now, she would be marrying the man she really loved. But he had, as far as a man can say such a thing, said that he did not love her. He liked her.

Did one ever find happiness in a marriage where one loved without return? Was there not, on the contrary, a very special and poignant suffering implicit in the very meaning of the phrase?

But if she did not marry him, he would go away.

Quite simply, that was the alternative. And she knew that she could not face it.

There would be problems and anxieties to face, if he went away. There would be explanations and possibly reproaches. But none of these really weighed with Leslie. She got no further than the fact that if he went away from her, she simply could not bear it. That was what mattered. If he went away from her, she did not want to face life any more.

"Do you want to think it over until to-morrow?" he asked at last, and the sound of his voice made her start.

"No," she said a little hoarsely. "Oh, no." For at the suggestion of delay she was suddenly overwhelmed by panic in case *he* should change his mind, or say that, after all, they must not act without more thought. "I have made up my mind, Reid."

"Sure?"

"Quite sure." Her voice cleared, and she looked up and smiled at him. "I'll marry you."

"Darling, will you really?" He gave a half-incredulous little laugh, and kissed her upturned face. "I thought all that grave consideration couldn't end in anything but a refusal."

"I — I had to weigh up everything carefully."

"Of course."

She wished she had not said that then. It made her decision sound such a poor and passionless thing. In that moment she longed, from the bottom of her soul, for a breathless, reckless, glorious romance with Reid.

She felt her heart beat more quickly and her blood race in her veins at the thought of what it must be like to be the real object of his bold, generous, almost arrogant love.

But that was not for her. Only Caroline had been able to command that. She must be satisfied to be liked and admired.

In one last surge of panic, she almost drew back even then. But she steadied herself, and heard him say,

"When is it to be, my sweet? Alma has already lectured me on the grave responsibilities of a bridesmaid."

"What, you too?" Leslie laughed, and she was pleased to hear that it sounded a perfectly natural and self-possessed laugh. "She was here not an hour ago, telling me that I should upset all her plans for the term if I didn't make up my mind soon."

"Well, we can put her out of her misery now. And your father too," he added, as a good-humoured afterthought.

"Yes." Leslie thought of her mother's pathetically controlled anxiety, and her not very successful efforts to hide her longing for happier, safer times, when she didn't have to think of money — or the lack of it — every hour of the day.

"I suppose we may as well make it soon, then." She tried so hard to make her tone cool and judicial that she succeeded in making it flat and indifferent.

So much so that she must have piqued him, for he

laughed a little angrily and, catching her in his arms, exclaimed,

" 'May as well' is no term to use to your bride-groom, you cold little fish! This *is* going to be a marriage, you know. Not a business assignment."

"Yes. I — I know."

"And I'll stake my male pride on your finding it a bit more interesting than you seem to think," he added almost threateningly, although he was laughing. "When do you marry me, eh?" And, bending her back lightly against his arm, he gave her a long, hard kiss on her mouth.

"Reid!" She struggled free.

"Don't you like it?"

"I——" She liked it so desperately that she was afraid she could not hide how much. "Of course, but — I can't very well answer your question if you go on kissing me like that."

"It has been done." He was suddenly in a remark-ably good humour. "But we'll take one thing at a time, if you like. When are you going to marry me?"

"Next — next month."

She had nearly said "next week," because when he held her and kissed her as he had just now, it was almost impossible not to say exactly what was in her mind. But she retained enough self-control to produce a reasonable answer. An answer which would show that she was ready to play her part, and yet not be-tray the wild eagerness and rapture which shook her at the very thought of being married to him.

"Next month——" He repeated her answer thought-fully. "Fine. Early next month?"

"If you like." But she smiled at him, to show that she "liked" also.

It was perfectly safe to like. Only one must not love.

They told the rest of the family later that evening, and received approving congratulations all round. In-deed, to Leslie, in her secret, frightened joy, it seemed that these were the only congratulations that mat-tered. The earlier ones, when she had first become engaged, had not meant anything. This was the real thing now. More real than even Reid guessed.

"It wasn't anything I said, was it, darling?" her mother asked anxiously when she got Leslie alone. "I mean — you aren't hurrying things on more than you want just because I poured out my worries to you?"

"No, Mother. It's all right." Leslie was very calm and tranquil about that. "The idea of an early wedding was — was Reid's. And I found I liked it very much indeed."

"I'm so glad! I'm so terribly glad for you — and so relieved for your father," she added naïvely.

Leslie smiled.

"Yes. He looked as though it were his own wedding, when we started to tell him of our decision."

"Well, I can tell you why now, dear. Why he and I are so specially relieved and delighted. We heard from the nursing home today — from Sir James. He does think there is a very reasonable chance that Morley may even walk again, if we can afford to let him go in for a long and expensive course of almost experimental treatment."

"Mother! How marvellous! Why didn't you tell me before?"

"Because — I'm ashamed to say it — our acceptance did depend on Reid giving his full financial support——"

"But he'd promised that anyway!" Leslie cried impatiently.

"Yes, I know. But I don't need to explain your father's attitude all over again."

"No, indeed!" Leslie laughed protestingly.

"Well, since you know his rather unreasonable views so well, you can see that what the situation amounted to was that the beginning of Morley's treatment more or less depended on the date of your wedding. I didn't want you to know that, Leslie, until you had decided your own future on personal considerations. We owed that to you, my dear. But I can't

122

tell you how glad I am that you have finally decided for an early marriage."

"I'm glad too," Leslie said soberly. "For Morley's sake as well as my own."

"There'll be a lot to arrange in a very short time, of course." But her mother sounded pleased, rather than harassed, by the prospect, Leslie noticed, and she guessed that wedding preparations were very dear to her mother's ingenuous and rather extravagant heart.

"We want things rather quiet, you know," she said, but she smiled indulgently at her mother.

"Of course, dear, of course."

But a look of enjoyable vagueness was beginning to come into Mrs. Greeve's beautiful dark eyes, and Leslie thought,

"She's beginning to think in dozens! I'll have to keep a curb on her. If Reid is going to pay out all that money for Morley, I'm not going to have him saddled with the expense of an extravagant trousseau for me."

Reid, however, had different views. Or so it turned out when she broached the subject to him and warned him to be firm on the question.

"Why shouldn't you have a swell trousseau?" he wanted to know. "Don't you like pretty clothes just as much as the next girl?"

"Of course. But that isn't the point."

"It's quite a good point, so far as I am concerned."

"But, Reid, in the circumstances, it's faintly dishonest. They will try to spend a lot of *your* money on what is, after all, *our* obligation. I don't mind exploiting you, or anyone else, for the sake of Morley's health. But I don't want an extravagant outfit at your expense."

He grinned at her.

"Don't you? I rather like the idea, personally."

"It's — it's not strictly necessary." She looked faintly put out.

"It doesn't have to be," he assured her. "I hope

you don't regard me as the sort of man who sees his bride only in terms of strict necessity."

She laughed reluctantly.

"Sweetheart," he said, "you haven't had much fun out of your marriage affairs up to now. Relax and enjoy yourself for the next month. Regard your parents as the inheritors of at least half of the Tabitha fortune, and shop accordingly. The bills will be paid, I promise you, and it doesn't much matter through whose banking account they pass. It's the same money. And if we stop to work out each time whose money it really is, we're none of us going to enjoy any of it."

There was a good deal of common sense in this — as in most of Reid's flippant utterances — and in the end Leslie accepted his advice.

Her mother — completely reassured by this new mood — accompanied her to London on a whirlwind shopping tour, and there, of course, they took every opportunity to see Morley.

To both of them it was obvious that he was already a different person. Hopeful, even confident, he greeted them like a man who *expected* everything to go well. Except for an occasional characteristically dry remark, there was no trace of that good-humoured but cynical melancholy which had distinguished him for so many years, and Leslie and her mother could hardly hide their joy at the change.

Afraid even then to raise too many hopes, they both at first avoided speaking much of the future. But Morley, to their surprise, showed no such reserve.

"I'm sorry I can't be at your wedding, Leslie dear," he said. "But I promise to be in circulation before the first christening, and if you'll make me godfather to the Reid heir, I'll undertake to carry out my duties as actively as the best."

She laughed rather tenderly at that, and the tenderness was not all for Morley.

"It's a bargain," she promised.

"How does Father get on with his prospective son-in-law now?" Morley asked with candour.

"Very well," Leslie assured him.

"Even to the extent of agreeing to accept half his fortune?"

That was the old Morley, and his mother murmured a not very convincing protest.

"Oh, yes. I think they are thrashing that out with Father's lawyers while we are away. And you needn't be deprecating about it, Mother," Leslie said. "Reid's perfectly right in saying that Father had a moral claim on part of the fortune. The only difficulty was in devising the exact circumstances in which Father would agree to see it in that way."

It was Morley who laughed indulgently that time.

"Well, I hope someone has managed to convey to Reid how grateful I am," he said more soberly. "Whatever moral rights there may be about the division of this inheritance, Reid would have been perfectly within his rights to hold on to the lot. And I'm well aware that, actually or figuratively, he has financed the miracle that's going to put me on my feet again."

His sister glanced at him affectionately.

"It's all right, Morley. I conveyed all that to him."

"Ye-es." Her brother looked at her with a certain amount of amused indulgence. "I suppose you certainly chose the best way possible of expressing the family gratitude. Happy, Leslie?"

"Divinely happy."

"It's queer — I thought I knew you so well. I was certain you were very much in love with Oliver."

"So was I. Certain, I mean."

"And it was a mistake?"

"Not in the sense that I misread my feelings at the time. I *was* very romantic about him. Particularly when I was a good deal younger." Both her mother and brother smiled indulgently at that. "But I suppose it was the old story of being in love with love — and the most attractive man I knew well at that time. After Reid came, there — wasn't anyone else."

"A good thing it was Oliver that Caroline fancied, then, and not Reid," observed Morley with candour.

"Thanks a lot! You mean you wouldn't back me in any competition?"

"Not against Caroline, my love," her brother insisted teasingly. "She's a natural winner in any feminine competition. In the slightly *démodé* expression — which has not, however, been successfully replaced — she's got what it takes." '

"And I haven't?"

He was surprised as well as amused, she saw, by the sharpness with which she said that.

"We-ell, it isn't a quality which brothers usually detect in their own sisters, you know. Only in other people's sisters."

"He's teasing you, Leslie dear," her mother put in peaceably. "You know perfectly well that Morley thinks the world of you."

"Say, rather, that Reid thinks the world of her, Mamma," Morley corrected, with a smile. "At the moment, his is the only opinion which interests Leslie — and quite rightly so."

"Well, he does think the world of her. Otherwise, why would he do all he has done?"

"You see, Leslie?" Morley smiled at her, still teasing, but with a great deal of affection too. "And remember that he had known the fatal Caroline once — and still he chose you."

"But suppose——" began Leslie. Then she stopped. Not only because of the amused lift of her brother's eyebrows, but because she realized with dismay that she had almost stumbled into the fatal mistake of demanding reassurance.

She changed the subject — laughed off the conversation as though she found it no more than the light-hearted teasing which Morley had meant it to be. But she was disturbed, and took herself to task afterwards.

"That's the danger in any marriage where one feels insecure," she thought remorsefully. "I *must* accept, and be thankful for, what I have. Not try to find reassurance of what doesn't really exist in any careless word that someone likes to utter."

She was glad she had identified this danger so early, and she imagined she was safely armed against it, now that she recognized it. Just as she was pretty sure, while she was in London and regarding Reid from a distance, that she could learn to achieve a nice balance in her relationship with him.

There was no reason why she should not show an easy, pleasant affection to him. That he would expect. All she must guard against was any display of the inner, breathless rapture which alternately enchanted and tormented her.

It should not be too difficult, she told herself.

But when she saw him again for the first time, after nearly a week's absence, it was all she could do not to throw herself into his arms and cling to him.

In her effort to appear self-contained, she threatened to turn their reunion into a very tame affair. But, fortunately, Reid had a natural talent for love-making — whether flirtatious or serious — and he greeted her in a manner that must not only have satisfied any member of the family who was by, but which reminded her of his gay boast that she should find their marriage rather more interesting than she seemed to expect.

Alma, who was a weekly boarder at a school in Pencaster, was at home on this occasion, as it was a Saturday, and when she said to Leslie, "Only two more weekends until your wedding," it seemed to give an exciting reality to the whole thing which, until now, it had lacked.

"Yes. I — find it hard to believe," Leslie confessed.

"Why?" the literal-minded Alma wanted to know.

"Well, I suppose any big and wonderful change is always rather difficult to accept in advance."

"I can always believe in anything I *want* to believe in," Alma asserted argumentatively. "Have you settled where you're going for your honeymoon yet?" For she resented that there had been a certain amount of reticence over the discussion of this.

"I don't know about the first part." Leslie smiled. "But later we are going to Laintenon."

"Where Great-Aunt Tabitha lived?"

"Yes."

"I say! She had a fabulous sort of villa there, didn't she? Will you stay there?"

"I doubt it. The place must be very big, and most of it would have been out of use for many years. It would be rather melancholy."

To Reid, Leslie said,

"Alma's just been asking where we are going to spend the first part of our honeymoon. I told her, quite truly, that I don't know. We can go to Laintenon after the first week or ten days, of course, but we still haven't settled on the first part."

"What about Paris?"

"Oh, no!" she cried sharply, remembering what Caroline had said about Paris, and how she had looked as she said it.

Reid regarded her thoughtfully, and she found herself blushing, and hoping wildly that he did not remember the occasion too.

There were few things that Reid forgot, however. He made no attempt to ask her why she objected so strongly to Paris. He merely said,

"Have you ever been to Italy?"

"No."

"Would you like that?"

"Very much," she said eagerly. Caroline had no associations with Italy, so far as she knew.

"Not one of the obvious places, like Rome or Florence. We might go to Verona, and we could hire a car and I'd take you round Lake Garda." He was speaking thoughtfully, as though he already visualized the scene and liked it.

"That sounds lovely," she said softly, anxious to make up for her slip over Paris. Besides, it did sound lovely.

"We could go to Venice for a day or two, if you liked."

"Yes. I should — love that."

"All right. I'll see after the arrangements. We'll fly to Milan and go on from there."

"Reid——"

"Yes?" He had been turning away, but he looked back at her now, over his shoulder.

"You didn't specially want to go to Paris, did you?"

"No, my sweet." He smiled full at her, and she found it very reassuring. "I want to go some place that you would like equally well. It's your honeymoon too, you know."

"Oh — thank you. I've always wanted to go to Italy."

That was true, and she hoped he would take it as sufficient reason for her almost violent refusal of Paris.

"Well, you're going now," he told her. "And I hope you'll have every reason to enjoy it."

She hoped so too — passionately. Hoped there would be no unforeseen crisis. Hoped that when people said a honeymoon could be more of an ordeal than an enjoyment, they were just being cynical. Hoped that somehow — somehow — when she took this terrible glorious risk, she would find that she had gambled on her happiness and won.

During the last days before her wedding, Leslie achieved a sort of detachment. She was the one in the household who usually shouldered most of the real work in any arrangements made, and her own wedding was no exception.

"You're so cool about everything — one would think it was someone else's wedding," Katherine said.

To which Leslie replied that she liked things done well, even at her own wedding.

"Leave her alone. She's just so sure of her happiness that she doesn't need to bother about anything else," her mother declared indulgently.

"But she *is* bothering about everything else," protested Katherine amusedly. "That's just it. She attends to every detail, so calmly and efficiently."

"Because she hasn't any inner worries," her mother explained. "That's it, isn't it, darling?"

Leslie said that was exactly what it was. And her mother looked peculiarly satisfied.

When her dress was sent home, the day before the wedding, she spread it out on the bed, and all the family — even her father — came to inspect it.

To be sure, he only said, "Very handsome, very handsome," in a modest tone, as though he were personally responsible for it, and then walked off. But her mother and her two sisters hung over it, exclaiming and admiring.

Leslie stood a little way back in the room, answering their remarks at random, gazing fascinatedly at the dress and thinking,

"When I put that dress on tomorrow, I shall be going to the church to marry Reid. I couldn't turn back now, if I wanted to. I'm absolutely committed. If I've made a terrible mistake, I can't do anything about it now."

"You do like it, don't you?" Katherine looked up and across the room at her.

"I adore it!"

"Oh — you were so quiet, I wondered if you were disappointed. Though I couldn't imagine how anyone could be."

"I think it's the loveliest wedding dress anyone ever had," Leslie said deliberately.

Her mother gave a pleased laugh.

"You'd better tell Reid that, darling. He told me I was to spare no expense whatever in finding you the dress of your dreams."

"He said that?" She flushed delightedly.

"He certainly did."

"Oh——" She laughed suddenly and felt indescribably happy. For surely no man thought or spoke on those lines, if his heart were completely set on another girl.

Why should she not hope and believe in her future

happiness? Why should not Reid recover from his infatuation for Caroline, just as she herself had grown out of her youthful passion for Oliver?

Looking back afterwards, she was always glad to remember that nothing spoilt the tranquil joy of her own wedding.

Worries there might have been beforehand. Problems there might be afterwards. But, during the service, and the small, intimate family reception which followed, she was quietly and completely happy.

"I don't think I ever saw anyone look so happy as you did," Katherine said to her, as she helped her sister change into her going-away suit of grey, edged with squirrel. "Once or twice, in the beginning, you know, I felt anxious about you. I thought maybe you were taking Reid for family reasons, in spite of all your protests. But when I saw the way you looked as you came down the aisle after the ceremony, I knew it was all right."

"Oh, Kate! Was it so obvious?"

"You bet it was! And quite right too," Katherine said, giving her a hug. "Have a wonderful time in Italy. But I'm sure you will. Reid's the kind to give any girl a wonderful time. What a good thing Caroline What's-her-name went and snaffled old Oliver, or you might have got yourself tied up with him."

"I don't think I should have. It simply *had* to be Reid," Leslie insisted. And in that moment she was actually grateful to Caroline for having taken Oliver off her hands.

Such are the beautiful, arrogant heights to which happiness can lift us.

It was over at last. They had run the gauntlet of parental blessing (her father), a few sentimental but happy tears (her mother), and an ill-directed shower of confetti (Alma). And they were in the car on the way to London, where they were to spend the night, and take the early morning plane to Milan the next day.

They drove through the bright, early autumn afternoon, past orchards where apples and pears hung heavy on the trees, and fields where the dark golden corn was being stacked. And Leslie thought the world had never been more beautiful, and that it was not humanly possible to be more happy than she.

"How did you enjoy your wedding, my sweet?" Reid asked at last, and she was aware that they must have been silent for a long time.

"I loved it."

He laughed.

"Girls always like weddings, I understand. Even other people's."

"Maybe. But one's own is always something special."

"Why, yes, I suppose it is. Even——" He stopped, because a big car was racing towards them, and he had to take the bend carefully.

"Rash idiot," he remarked to Leslie, when they were past.

"Yes. But — what were you saying, Reid?"

"Something in general praise of weddings, wasn't I? Good heavens, just look at that orchard. Heaviest crop we've seen so far."

She stared at the orchard, and hated its mellow beauty. But she managed to say something appropriate. And — much harder — she managed not to yield to the temptation of forcing him back on to the subject they had so abruptly left.

What was the qualification he had been going to make, with such careless matter-of-factness, about their own wedding? Until they reached London, and the hotel where they were to stay, the question tormented her.

In the luxury hotel where Reid had assumed she would like to stay, a very beautiful suite had been reserved. And so obviously pleased was he to be providing her with the very best of everything on her honeymoon that she had to conceal from him, at all costs, her dismay at discovering how very palatial and un-intimate the suite was.

There were two bedrooms and a sitting-room — which seemed excessive for one night, Leslie could not help thinking. And, for the first time, the dreadful idea came to her that perhaps he still regarded their marriage as a friendly compromise rather than an actual fact.

Was this his tactful way of indicating that the wedding need not radically change the relationship between them for the time being?

She told herself that she was being fanciful. And then that — even if she had guessed right — she must be patient. The family necessity had forced them into a seeming intimacy for which he might think neither of them was ready.

"But, if he thinks that, how am I to make him see otherwise?" she thought desperately. "And, if I can't make him see it, how am I to bear it?"

They had arrived too late for dinner. But they had supper together in the brilliant, beautiful restaurant, and danced for a while afterwards to a superb band. But, all the while, this new and terrible problem hovered in the back of her consciousness and, try as she would, she could not be at ease with him.

"Well, we're due at the air office at a fiendishly early hour in the morning," he said at last. "It's about time we turned in, isn't it, and got what sleep we can?"

"I expect so."

"Would you like a drink before you go up?"

"No, thank you."

She wondered if she sounded as cold and casual to him as she did to herself. She thought perhaps she must have, because he gave her an amused, rather quizzical glance as he patted her shoulder, and said,

"All right. I think I will. Good night, my sweet. Sleep well. I'll see you tomorrow morning about six."

"Good night," she said, and went calmly towards the lift. And no one — least of all Reid — could have guessed that her heart was dead within her.

CHAPTER TEN

"NO SMOKING! Fasten Safety Belts!" ordered the electric sign at the front of the aeroplane cabin. And Leslie, occupied though she was with her own private problem, could not suppress an instinctive thrill of excitement at this indication that her first flight was about to begin.

"All right?" Reid, in the seat beside her, smiled at her as the plane bowled forward over the field, bumping over the unevenness of the ground with a slow clumsiness which completely concealed the grace and speed which would distinguish it as soon as it was in the air.

"Yes, of course." She smiled back at him. For was not their relationship one of pleasant friendliness? "I'm terribly excited, that's all."

He laughed indulgently and patted her hand, reminding her yet again of the time he had done that when first they met.

How angry she had been with him, that afternoon when he first asked her the way to Cranley Magna. She remembered exactly the feel of his long, strong brown hand on hers then, and how she had resented the familiarity.

Now she loved to have him touch her. She loved everything about him, if only——

"We're off," he said. And she realized that they had left the ground without her even noticing the fact.

It was a perfectly smooth flight, almost monotonous in its early uneventfulness, until they began to cross the Alps.

Leslie thought that never in her life had she seen anything so beautiful as the scene spread below her. The blues and purples of the mountain shadows, with the jewel-like gleam of a lake here and there. The great snowy peaks, gilded by the midday sunshine, rising on every hand. The green of thick vegetation in the valleys, when they came low enough to pick that out. And even an occasional stream and waterfall.

It was like some immense and beautiful toy, viewed from this height, and to look down upon it gave one an almost godlike sense of detachment and wonder.

"Oh, Reid! I'm so glad we came!" she exclaimed.

And he laughed and said, "I'm glad too. It's wonderful, isn't it?"

She wanted to ask if he had ever looked down on this scene, or any similar one, with Caroline. But she knew that even so prosaic a honeymoon as he evidently intended theirs to be could be ruined by a few foolish questions or comments. Caroline was definitely a subject to be left alone.

They arrived in Milan in time for lunch. But, as they had decided to go on to Verona the same day, there was time for little more than a stroll through the Galleria, a glance at the Scala and a breathless few minutes before the beauty of the Cathedral.

Then they were on their way again, this time by train.

It was Leslie's first journey abroad, and she was fascinated by every detail. Just to have people round her talking a beautiful and unfamiliar language was exciting. And, since Reid appeared to know enough Italian to deal with most emergencies, she was able to enjoy the novelty of it all without any of the minor anxieties which usually beset an inexperienced traveller.

It was early evening by the time they reached Verona, but there was still enough light for Reid to point out the main features as they drove to their hotel.

Sharply etched against the evening sky, and dominating the town, rose the great broken arches of the Roman amphitheatre, and Reid promised her that they would explore this on the following day.

"We're too late for the season of open-air opera that they do here in the summer," he said. "But you'll still have plenty of more informal music in the open-air cafés around the centre of the town."

"It's fascinating!" She was glancing eagerly from side to side at the curious, almost mediaeval streets through which they were passing. And when they drew up at their hotel, she thought the place looked more like a rather broken-down palace than any hotel she had ever been in.

There was nothing in the nature of palatial suites in this hotel. No private sitting-room. But they were shown into a couple of pleasant rooms, with a communicating door. And when the porter pulled up the green slatted sun-blinds, Leslie looked out into a romantic-looking courtyard, where vines were growing, and a beautiful, brown-skinned youth was twanging some stringed instrument and singing "O Sole Mio."

It was all very picturesque and intriguing.

"How do you like it?"

They had been left alone now, and Reid had come in from his room to look round hers and see that she had everything she wanted.

"It's enchanting. Do you think the boy out there is a special stage 'effect'? Or did he just happen to be there?"

"Oh, just happened, I expect." Reid went to the window and leant out to exchange a few laughing words with the boy, who almost immediately broke into the poignantly gay strains of "Marechiare."

"It's delightful at first," Reid said. "They're a bit inclined to keep it up to all hours, but that's all part of the life here. Nearly everyone goes to sleep in the middle of the day because it's so hot, and that means that they stay up late into the night. Even the children. You'll see, when we go out to get something to eat."

"Aren't we dining at the hotel, then?"

"No, no. It's more fun out of doors."

She agreed that it would be.

"Give me twenty minutes to wash and change,

136

and I'll be ready for anything," she promised. "I must get into something cooler."

"But take a coat," he warned, as he went back into his own room. "It gets cold very suddenly."

As she changed, she hummed a soft accompaniment to the song outside and felt her spirits lighten. The faintly fantastic atmosphere here, so unlike anything she had ever known before, seemed to whisper to her that anything could happen, after all.

The warm night air, the music and something else quite indefinable seemed to combine to create a sense of drama and romance, and, like everyone else who has ever known the beauty of Romeo and Juliet's city, Leslie fell a victim then and there to the purple twilight of Verona and the spell which it casts.

"There's something about this place, Reid!" she declared, when she joined him later, cool and enchanting in a flowered silk dress, patterned in vivid blues and greens against a white background, which seemed to accentuate her fairness and make her look very young.

"Sure. That's what Romeo thought, I guess," Reid agreed, smiling his approval as he took her coat from her and tossed it over his arm.

"Do we take a taxi?"

"No. We walk. Everyone walks here, in the centre of the town. Lots of the streets haven't even got a separate pavement and road."

So they strolled through the chattering, laughing, flirting crowds who thronged the streets, until they came to the great Piazza Bra, where, sure enough, a band was playing, and under the artificial lights the trees and plants in the gardens looked like something on a stage.

Couples strolled arm in arm in the darker paths of the gardens, plump, motherly-looking peasant women sat on the benches and knitted and gossiped as though it were early afternoon. And everywhere the dark-eyed, golden-skinned "bambini" tumbled and played and laughed and cried and got in everyone's way.

"They ought to be in bed, surely!" Leslie exclaimed. "They're just babies."

"They've done a good deal of sleeping during the heat of the day, I expect," Reid said. "They enjoy the cool as much as anyone else now. And if it seems an odd way to bring up children, by our standards, they none of them seem any the worse for it."

That was true enough. Leslie thought she had never seen prettier, happier children. And presently, when she and Reid sat down at a table on the pavement and proceeded to have their supper, she divided her attention almost equally between her excellent meal and the charming, amusing children, who appeared to be kissed or slapped with equal impartiality by their fond parents.

Gradually any sense of time slipped away. One had the absurd and pleasant feeling that one could go on like this all night. And when, after a while, they rose to go, Reid said,

"You don't want to go in yet, do you?"

"Oh, no. I feel I should be missing something." He laughed.

"We'll stroll some more." No one seemed to think in terms of anything more hurried here. "And I'll show you one or two places that we can glance at now and explore better by daylight."

As they walked along, he slipped his arm round her, partly to keep her near him when they came to crowded places, and partly because it seemed the natural way for couples to walk if they were young and happy.

She looked up at him and laughed a little, responding to the pressure of his arm with an eagerness she would not probably have shown if they had been at home in England.

"Decided you aren't frightened of me, after all?" he enquired, with an air of not unkindly teasing.

"Frightened of you! I've never been frightened of you," declared Leslie with truth.

"Oh, yes. You were frightened of me yesterday evening. Kept on giving me nervous, wide-eyed looks, until I began to feel like the villain of the piece who'd threatened to ruin the old homestead if the heroine didn't come to heel."

"Reid! I've never looked like that in my life."

"Then what was the trouble yesterday?"

"Why, I — I—— There wasn't any."

He didn't dispute that. He let them walk in silence for a few moments longer. Then he said, quite gently,

"Do you feel this marriage is a little too much for you in some ways, honey?"

"No, Reid." She spoke softly, but without hesitation. "Not in any way at all.".

"Not even if I tell you that no man would bring his wife to Verona, of all places, and not expect to make love to her?"

"Not even then." She was smiling, and some of the sweet confidence which had come to her during her wedding returned to her now.

He laughed softly, and bent his head to kiss the side of her cheek — a proceeding which was watched with approval and no surprise whatever by a plump, elderly Italian who was passing.

"Aren't you going to tell me what was wrong yesterday?"

"Just that I thought — when I saw that great suite — and you were rather matter-of-fact about everything — and I remembered about — Caroline——"

"Why the hell do you want to quote Caroline at this moment?" he demanded, but not angrily.

"I don't! It was just that—— Oh, I didn't *know* how you regarded me, Reid. I got nervous, if you like. But only in case you had some idea that the marriage was truly just one of convenience, and — and—"

"You've been reading too many modern novels, my sweet, all about people who behave any way but the normal one," Reid assured her good-humouredly. "You don't really think any man would marry anything as pretty and sweet as you are, and then decide to be brotherly, do you?"

She laughed, even a little more than the occasion demanded. For, out of the past, there had risen the ridiculous memory of Oliver saying she was like a sister to him. It had hurt so unbearably at the time, and now it hurt no longer.

And with that memory went the further recollection that she had drawn some sort of comparison even then, and told herself that in no circumstances whatever would Reid regard her as a sister.

"It's all right," she said happily. "I expect I was silly and fanciful. It isn't always easy to — to understand someone else's reactions, even when you know them very well."

"And you consider that you know me very well?"

"Pretty well."

"But you're satisfied with the idea that you should know me better." It was almost a statement, rather than a question.

"Yes, Reid," she said, and for a moment he tightened his arm round her.

Then he paused to point out to her the beauties of some twelfth-century church they were passing, and they didn't talk any more about their inmost feelings or reactions. They might have been any couple of interested tourists taking their first enchanted look at one of the old Italian cities.

Except that there was a glow of happiness in her face not achieved by all tourists.

They stayed in Verona for about ten days, visiting Venice and Padua, and hiring a car sometimes and driving out to Lake Garda when it became too hot to be comfortable on the plains.

If the scene had been dull and humdrum and the weather disastrous, Leslie would still have thought it the most wonderful place in the world, and this the most wonderful holiday. For in her new-found happy intimacy with Reid she had discovered, it seemed to her, an entirely new meaning to life.

She had always been of a reasonably happy nature, and her home background had been — in spite of Morley's tragedy and her father's weaknesses — a very contented one. But it seemed to her now that all the years before she had known Reid had a pleasantly negative quality. She had been happy, of course. As happy as she knew how to be then.

But as Reid's wife she had discovered a source and spring of such radiant, positive happiness that she sometimes wondered how she had been able to bear life before she knew him.

She made no attempt to discuss it with him. To do so would have been to betray more to him than she felt she safely could as yet. But she could not know him as well as she did now without realizing that he too was happy.

How far it went with him, she could not tell. His relationship with her might well supply no more than the "negative content" she had known herself before she met him. It was possible that for him the heights could only be touched with Caroline.

So far as Leslie was concerned, they could have stayed there for weeks. But one morning, when they were idling happily over their breakfast of coffee and rolls, creamy butter and cherry jam, their post was brought to them, and Reid's included a letter which had been forwarded on from France.

"I think we'll have to push on to Laintenon soon, my sweet," he said, frowning a little over the letter. "There are quite a number of things to settle still. This letter is from Aunt Tabitha's lawyers, to remind me that, when I dashed off to England, I left a good deal undone."

"Well——" She looked up, smiling, from an originally spelt bulletin of Alma's. "Whenever you say. However long I stay, I shan't really want to leave here. But no honeymoon can go on for ever."

"The honeymoon doesn't have to stop, just because we shift the scene," he reminded her.

"No? Maybe not."

But she privately thought that neither Laintenon, nor any other place, would ever hold for her the charm and magic of this city where she had first come to know Reid as her husband.

"I'll go and enquire about train times." Reid got up. "Don't hurry. Stay and finish your breakfast — and your post."

"There's an incredible epistle from Alma which you'll enjoy later. I never knew anyone more naturally resistant to education. Her spelling's a disgrace," Leslie remarked indulgently. "But I see there's a letter from Kate too. That should have all the local gossip."

When Reid had gone, she poured herself out another cup of coffee, and prepared to enjoy Katherine's letter at her leisure.

Katherine, for all her slightly languid beauty, was a clear-headed young woman, and always gave her news crisply and in what Leslie mentally called the right order of importance. Her letters were almost invariably a pleasure, because she told one exactly what one most wanted to know.

This one was no exception. In two pages, she had given Leslie a satisfactory account of the family's affairs, and left her with the pleasant impression that life at Cranley Magna was easier and less problematical than it had been for many a long day.

In addition, she was able to report that Morley made continuously satisfactory progress, and that, within a week or so, the great effort was to be made to put him literally on his feet again.

Even to read about it brought such a lump into Leslie's throat that, for a moment, she laid down the page and looked away across the sunny piazza with tears in her eyes.

Dear Morley! who had been so patient and so uncomplaining. If he really regained the use of his legs, she thought she would never be able to ask more of heaven again. That — and to have Reid too! It was almost too much.

She picked up the last sheet of the letter, and in this Katherine had arrived at the general local gossip, as distinct from family news.

I met Mrs. Bendick the other day (she wrote). Our Mrs. B., I mean — not Oliver's glamorous lady. She told me that they didn't have more than about four days' honeymoon (I was glad to be able to report that you did much better) because Oliver hadn't any more holiday due to him at that time.

However, he has had his release now, and they're off somewhere else, to make up for the short time they had in the beginning. Mrs. B. wagged her head and tut-tutted a bit about her new daughter-in-law. I think she considers C. rather a bird of paradise for any man to keep happily cooped up in an ordinary domestic pen. And I must say I agree with her.

Still, we won't look for trouble. Oliver's very steadiness may appeal to her, though personally I should have thought Reid was more her type. Not that I wish to suggest your Reid lacks steadiness. But he's what the Victorians used to call "dashing" as well. And, unless I'm much mistaken, Caroline likes a little dash about her men.

Again Leslie put down the letter. But not with sympathetic tears in her eyes this time. She looked away across the piazza again, it was true, but now there was a thoughtful look in her eyes and they were a little narrowed. Like the eyes of someone who strives to see something just out of range.

Kate was smart, of course. She would see unerringly that Reid was more Caroline's type of man than Oliver was.

And yet — Caroline had chosen Oliver.

If only one could be sure that she had chosen him coolly and with judgment. If one could be certain that there had been no element of pique, or disappointment, in her choice.

"But I shall never know that now," thought Leslie.

"And I shall be a fool if I let my thoughts dwell on it."

She wondered if Reid sometimes went over and over the past in his own mind. He must, she supposed. And if he wondered uneasily whether Caroline had made her choice out of little more than pique, the reflection must cause him even more disquiet than it did her.

It was at that moment that Leslie took a very firm decision for the future.

When she and Reid finally settled in England they would not, she determined, make their home anywhere near Cranley Magna or, still less, Pencaster.

She would be terribly sorry not to be near the family, of course, and she knew that they probably expected that her future home would be at any rate within easy reach of them. She hated to have to admit so much fear of any woman — Caroline or anyone else — but there were risks which one should not take. Better to face the fact, and act accordingly, rather than ignore a known danger and pretend that bravado and pride could take one past it.

Reid — and Oliver too — were, she was sure, the stuff of which faithful husbands are made. And, little though she wished to pay tributes to Caroline, she had no reason to think the girl was a wilful trouble-maker.

But the whole situation was alive with danger. And when emotional gunpowder was lying around, only a fool struck matches.

By the time Reid came back, with the news that they could set off on their journey to Laintenon on the morrow, she had finished her coffee, read Katherine's letter and put it away in her handbag, and was ready to divert Reid with Alma's illiterate epistle.

"Had Kate any news?" he asked, looking up once, with a laugh, from Alma's letter.

"Just general family gossip, and a cautiously expressed hope that Morley might try to walk sometime next week."

144

"Good work! Don't get excited in advance, sweetheart, in case there's a disappointment. But, if it's a success, we'll have a long-distance call from Laintenon, and you can talk to Kate and hear all about it."

She smiled at him. He thought of everything.

But she hoped he would not think of ensuring that they settled near her family in case she became homesick.

The next day they left Italy, and it was not until the early afternoon of the following day that they arrived at Laintenon. Laintenon was about ten miles in from the coast, and so exactly like what Leslie had always supposed a French country town would be that she could have laughed aloud with amusement and delight.

It was a little bigger than she expected and, because of some rather famous health springs in the district, there were still a good many tourists, even though it was strictly out of the season.

For them, however, there was no question of difficulties of accommodation, even apart from Great-Aunt Tabitha's deserted villa. Reid drove straight to the tall, narrow house where he had lodged during the months he had lived in Laintenon, and was welcomed as a long-lost son by his voluble and sentimental landlady.

Leaving her to unpack, Reid went off immediately to see the lawyers and, with the aid of a good many gestures and a certain amount of schoolgirl French, Leslie managed to have a nice informative chat with Madame Blanchard.

Reid, she gathered, was all that was good, noble and generous, a reputation which he appeared to have established for himself during the year or so he lived there.

No one, it seemed, was better pleased than Madame Blanchard when *"ce cher Monsieur Carté"* (which was her version of Reid's name) had inherited a great fortune from the mysterious old lady who lived in the Villa Rossignol.

No — she didn't know why it was called that. There had never been any nightingales there in her time. But perhaps when the old lady first came there as a bride there might have been. That would be seventy years ago or more.

The old lady had not been seen in the town for at least fifteen years before her death, but everyone said the villa was very handsome inside, and the grounds were beautiful, though out of condition now.

No doubt "Monsieur Carté" would be taking his bride to see the place. He had been very good to the old lady. Everyone agreed about that, and no one — if Madame Blanchard were to be believed — grudged him what she called his splendid inheritance.

Being naturally curious, she tried very hard (though with great politeness) to find out from Leslie how much the splendid inheritance had amounted to. But as Leslie really did not know, she was able to withhold this piece of information.

By the time Reid returned, Leslie and Madame Blanchard were firm friends.

"After we've had something to eat, we'll go up and have a look at the villa, if you like," Reid offered. "A good deal of the stuff won't be much good to us, and will hardly have even a sentimental value for anyone in your family. But you had better have a look at everything. A few of the things are very beautiful, as well as valuable."

Leslie was only too eager to accept the suggestion and, after an early dinner, they walked out in the cool of the evening to the Villa Rossignol, which stood about half a mile outside the town, almost hidden in a beautiful grove of cypress trees.

To Leslie, there was something melancholy, as well as intensely interesting, in this visit to the home of the legendary figure who had stood for so much in their family life.

The place must have been magnificent once, with the heavy magnificence of a past age. But now it was all so silent and dusty and lifeless. No one lived there any longer, except the elderly caretaker and his wife. And for years and years before that only an old lady, who had long outlived all her contemporaries, and a couple of ancient servants.

"It's hard to believe that *she* came here once as a happy, youthful bride, isn't it?" Leslie said, when they had seen all they wanted to see of the house itself, and were strolling through the vast, tangled gardens.

"I suppose it is." Reid held aside a great bunch of some sweet-smelling shrub so that Leslie could pass. "But she was quite happy, you know, even towards the end when she was getting tired and very old."

"Was she, Reid? You made her happy, didn't you?"

He smiled.

"I had something to do with it. She was a lively old lady, and used to say that she could still enjoy active life at second-hand. She used to like me to come up to the villa and talk to her — tell her stories of what I had done in the years before I came to Laintenon. I knocked about the world a good bit, you know, and she enjoyed a good story better than almost anyone I ever knew. I wish she could have seen you," he added suddenly. "She'd have liked you."

"Would she?" Leslie was indescribably gratified. "How do you know?"

"She used to say she knew the sort of girl I ought to marry. And she used to describe something very like you."

"She didn't like Caroline," thought Leslie, with inner conviction. "I suppose he brought her here once or twice, during their engaged days."

Ridiculously, she felt a sudden kinship with old Great-Aunt Tabitha, which had nothing whatever to do with their very flimsy relationship in fact. And she was very glad she had come to the villa and seen it for herself.

When they finally left the place, she was smiling a little, so that Reid put his arm round her as they walked down the hill to the town again. It reminded

147

her of the first magical evening in Verona, and she thought,

"I am going to be just as happy here."

She even wondered why she had been so foolish and so cowardly as to have doubted her happiness at any time, because everything seemed simple and secure now.

And then she looked up, and coming along the road towards them was Caroline, dressed in white and swinging a beach-hat by the strings, for all the world as though she had walked out specially to meet them.

CHAPTER ELEVEN

FOR A few seconds, Leslie stared at the advancing figure. Then she said in a queer, matter-of-fact little voice, "Why, there's — Caroline," almost as though she had been expecting her. As perhaps, in a way, she had.

"Caroline!" exclaimed Reid. Then he said, "Hell!" And for the first time since she had known him, Leslie detected a note of something like alarm in his voice.

By that time, Caroline had come right up with them, and she took off her sun-glasses and exclaimed, "Well, for heaven's sake! Look who's here. Where did you two spring from?"

And then she laughed. But she could afford to laugh, thought Leslie. It was not her life that was in ruins.

Then Leslie heard herself laugh too, and say something about ridiculous coincidences. So apparently she was doing quite well too. And Reid was joking and speaking in his usual half-flippant manner. Only his arm round Leslie's waist was uncomfortably tight.

"You're staying at your old place, I suppose?" Caroline looked at and spoke to Reid as someone who knew all his usual haunts and habits.

"Yes, of course. Madame Blanchard has gathered us both under her wing by this time. Where are you staying?"

"Oliver and I are renting the smallest villa ever. We were lucky to get it at a few days' notice, of course. It's not fifty yards along the road. You must come back with me for a drink."

Leslie would have given anything to say that unfortunately they were going on somewhere else. But they were not going anywhere else, and if she said they were, Reid — and perhaps Caroline too — would know that she was running away.

So they turned back and fell into step beside Caroline, who was busy explaining what Leslie already knew from Katherine's letter — that, as soon as Oliver's replacement arrived, they had decided to have the second instalment of their honeymoon.

"But why Laintenon?" Reid asked dryly.

"I had a fancy for it," Caroline retorted, and for a moment her strange, significant glance drifted over him, expressing something which Leslie felt she herself could not understand. "I knew how attractive it could be at this time of year, you see."

"Yes, of course."

Usually Reid's voice was full and expressive. Now it sounded flat and without any overtones.

They turned in at the gate of a small, white villa, set in a pretty formal garden, and Caroline led the way round to the back of the house. Here, sprawling comfortably in a deck chair on the verandah, was Oliver, looking exactly as though he were at home in Cranleymere.

To see his familiar figure in these utterly unfamiliar surroundings seemed so much the last touch of fantasy that Leslie began to think she must be in some dreadful sort of dream.

But there was nothing dreamlike about the way Oliver sprang to his feet at the sight of them, and came forward exclaiming with obvious pleasure.

There were the same incredulous questions and the same half-joking answers as there had been with Caroline, and everyone made at least a very good appearance of being delighted to see everyone else. And then Caroline said that she would bring drinks out on to the verandah, and suggested Leslie might like to come into the house and help her collect things.

They went indoors and, for the first time in their short acquaintance, Leslie realized, she and Caroline were alone together. Somehow the situation embarrassed her, though she hardly knew why. But evidently there was nothing in it to disturb Caroline.

She opened cupboards — still obviously unfamiliar

to her — and searched for what she wanted, and all the time she kept up a desultory stream of conversation.

It was natural for her to refer to Leslie's wedding, of course, but Leslie felt herself almost wince when Caroline remarked casually,

"In the end, Reid and you made nearly as much of a rush job of it as we did, didn't you?"

"Not quite. We did fix our wedding date about a month ahead, which gave me a little time for preparation. Here's the corkscrew, if that's what you're looking for."

"Oh, thanks." Caroline was arranging her tray with apparent carelessness but completely efficient result. "We settled things in a matter of days, in the end, you know."

"Yes, I know," Leslie said. "Why?"

The question — curt and almost rude though it might be — was out before Leslie could stop it.

But Caroline did not seem to mind. She laughed, with a sort of reminiscent amusement, and said,

"We had a row, as a matter of fact. And then a making-up. And — you know how these things are — suddenly we found ourselves arranging to get married the first moment we could. It's funny — quarrels sometimes clear the air, don't they?"

"Sometimes," Leslie agreed. "This isn't your — first visit to Laintenon, is it?"

"Oh, no. I was here in the days when I was engaged to Reid," explained Caroline, who had no inhibitions about past loves apparently.

"I see," said Leslie, who had. And then they went out into the garden again.

Both men sprang to their feet. But it was Reid who came to take the tray from Caroline. And Leslie called herself mean and petty because she could not help noticing that his hands almost closed over Caroline's as he did so.

Oliver, meanwhile, was setting a chair for her and asking her how she liked her first glimpse of France.

Again there was something completely unreal about

the scene. By every association of childhood and girlhood, she was much nearer to Oliver than she was to Reid. And, knowing, as she did, the link between Reid and Caroline, she could not help finding it horribly natural that they should be laughing over the same tray of drinks, while she paired off with Oliver.

It was like some stage comedy in which two couples had got mixed, but would probably sort themselves out in the last act.

"But what will the 'sorting out' amount to in our case?" she thought unhappily. And she looked at Oliver, very charmingly playing host to her, and wondered what she had ever seen in him.

Naturally, he was intensely interested in everything she had to tell him about Morley, and usually Leslie would have asked nothing better than to talk of her beloved brother. But all the time she was dreadfully aware of Reid and Caroline, sitting side by side, laughing and talking, recalling shared experiences and exchanging common allusions.

She knew she was being absurd. They were not saying a word which could not easily be heard by herself and Oliver, if they cared to suspend their own conversation and listen. It was impossible to suppose that they were indulging in any more than lively social chat. And yet, she could hardly keep her attention on her own talk with Oliver, and it was all she could do to look interested and natural.

Oliver did drop his voice once, but only to say, in the amused, teasing kind of way that is permissible between life-long friends,

"You solved the Aunt Tabitha problem very satisfactorily in the end, didn't you?"

"The—— Oh — oh, yes. Reid has been wonderfully generous."

"Someone taking my name in vain?" Reid looked up at that moment, and Leslie managed to smile at him quite naturally.

"I was only telling Oliver how generous you were over Great-Aunt Tabitha's fortune."

"What was that?" Caroline pricked up her ears. "I like to hear about fortunes. The trouble is — they never come my way."

There was an odd little silence. Then Leslie said, with a composure which surprised herself.

"Didn't Oliver ever tell you about my Great-Aunt Tabitha — and how we always expected her to leave her fortune to us, as a family?"

"No. Don't tell me there was nothing in the end. I couldn't bear it." Caroline smiled her lazy smile.

"She left it to Reid instead."

"Reid!" Caroline, who had been lounging in her chair, sat up suddenly. "Do you mean to say you had a fortune left to you, Reid, and never told me about it?"

"It was after your time, my sweet," Reid said composedly.

"I wish he wouldn't call her that," thought Leslie angrily. *"She* isn't his 'sweet' now."

"But tell me now." Caroline seemed extraordinarily interested. "Leslie's relation went and left you her money?"

"Well, she was — very remotely — related to both of us, you see. She was the old lady at the Villa Rossignol."

"No!" Caroline seemed really impressed. "Oh, oh! and I never bothered to make her like me when I was here. She might have left *me* something, if I had."

"Don't be such a shameless hussy," Oliver put in affectionately.

And Leslie thought, "They're both playing up to her now!"

Aloud, however, she only said,

"I'm surprised you never happened to tell Caroline our family story, Oliver."

"I thought she might set her cap at Reid and his fortune, if I did," Oliver replied promptly. "And see how right I was. She's displaying a dreadfully mercenary streak at the moment, aren't you, darling?"

"Well, no one likes to think they've let a fortune

slip," Caroline objected. "Leslie will sympathize with me, won't you, Leslie? She knows what it feels like to see a fortune vanish."

"She doesn't need to worry. She brought it back into the family again, by marrying my charming self," Reid pointed out.

"So *that* was it!"

Leslie dug her nails into the palms of her hands to keep herself calm and smiling. She *knew* they were all chaffing each other, and that there wasn't a word of serious meaning in the whole conversation. But oh, it was too near the hurtful truth! She felt she could hardly bear it.

And even as she told herself it was all just flippant nonsense, something deep down inside her protested that perhaps there was a grain of truth in it all.

Perhaps Caroline *would* have chosen differently, if she had known Reid was a very rich man.

But, in that case, why had Reid not told her? He had had opportunity enough. Or, if not, he could have made an opportunity. *His* silence was less understandable than Oliver's, now she came to think of it. And perhaps he was bitterly regretting his silence by now.

She told herself that she must leave the subject alone. That all these delvings into the recent past were dangerous. She thought she had convinced herself of the wisdom of this. And yet, when at last they were on the way home, almost the first thing she said to Reid was,

"Don't you think it was odd that Oliver hadn't told her — told Caroline, I mean — all about Great-Aunt Tabitha's leaving her fortune to you?"

"Not particularly." He grinned and switched lightly at the tall grass by the roadside with a stick he was carrying. "No man actually advertises the attractions of his rivals."

"He didn't know you were a rival of his," she said almost coldly.

"That's true. But he might have thought that news

154

of the inheritance would turn me into one," countered Reid, still smiling.

She longed to be able to smile and joke about it with him. Or else she longed for him to be serious about it with her. She was not quite sure which.

What she did know was that, however unwise it might be, she had to ask that other question — about his own reactions.

"Reid," she said, and she was glad that she kept her voice light and steady, "why didn't you tell her yourself? It — it might have made a difference."

"I didn't want to be married for my money, my love. We all like to preserve the fond illusion that we are loved for ourselves alone," he pointed out, still in the same half-laughing tone.

She didn't laugh, however. She said, slowly and almost sombrely,

"And you were very anxious for Caroline to love you for yourself alone, weren't you?"

He looked at her then, with a sharpened attention of which she was immediately aware. And when he spoke his voice was just a little dry.

"Look here, honey," he said, "do you really think there's any good purpose in raking up the past like this?"

"I didn't rake it up," she exclaimed bitterly. "It came to meet us, of its own accord. Oh, why did they have to choose here, of all the places in Europe? Why couldn't they have gone anywhere else?"

"Yes, I guess it was a nasty back-hander of Fate," he agreed. "But it might not be a bad thing, in the end, you know. There's something to be said for facing out a situation and taking stock of it, instead of perpetually running away from it."

"Oh, that's taking things too far! I didn't mind the thought of — of meeting them later on, in my own home circle. But here — on our honeymoon — the only other people in the place whom we know! It's — it's too much."

"Darling, I didn't realize it was so unpleasant for

you." He put out his hand towards her but, for the first time since she had said she would marry him, she flinched away angrily from the contact.

"No, don't touch me, or — or pet me! I couldn't bear it just now."

"All right," he said, in the most matter-of-fact tone possible, and they walked on in silence. A silence during which she was able to review her disastrous behaviour of the last ten minutes.

How could she have betrayed herself like that? How could she have lost her self-control so hopelessly? She had behaved like a jealous, over-fond creature, instead of the cool, intelligent companion she had tried to be to him.

What was he thinking now? Was he appalled at the revelation that she minded enough to be jealous?

He was sauntering along beside her, a little serious, but otherwise much as he usually was. But what was he thinking, what was he thinking?

"Reid," she said at last, "I'm awfully sorry. I don't know why I spoke the way I did. I——"

"That's all right, honey. There are no apologies called for," he interrupted. "This is one of the times when the less one says, the better one feels about it afterwards. I know it isn't easy for you, the way things have turned out."

For a terrible moment, she thought he meant that he had guessed how she felt about him.

And then, with a relief which almost made her laugh hysterically, she realized what was in his mind. He thought she was upset at seeing *Oliver* again.

It was perfectly natural that he should, of course. He was not to know that neither Oliver nor any man other than himself meant anything to her now. He was sorry she had had to watch what he believed to be the love of her life enjoying his honeymoon with someone else.

"Oh, Reid——" she began. And then she saw that he was indeed right when he said that the less they talked about it, the better. "Th-thank you for being so understanding," was all she ventured in the end. And he gave her a friendly smile and spoke of other things.

It was not until quite a long time afterwards that she wondered whether to have Oliver accepted as the reason for her distress were not almost worse than to have Reid suspect the truth.

She was saved, it was true, from the humiliation of having him know her real feelings. But, instead, Reid was confirmed in the belief that Oliver still remained as the man she loved.

"And I wanted so desperately for us to move gradually and naturally away from that!" she thought wretchedly. "I wanted him to feel that our marriage already meant enough to me for the situation to work out happily one day. Now — just as he is unsettled by his meeting Caroline again — I have given him the impression that the links between ourselves are very thin and unimportant after all."

She had even, in that final moment of nervous revulsion, implied that she quite hated any advance of his when Oliver was very much in her mind.

All the beauty and the happy confidence of their days in Verona seemed gone suddenly. They were very pleasant and friendly to each other — they even joked a little — but the inner sympathy and understanding was gone.

"If it ever existed," thought Leslie. "If it ever existed. Perhaps I just imagined that too, and the only real thing is the way he looks at Caroline, and the memories he has of her here."

During the next few days, she tried in every way she could to keep their relationship on an easy, almost conventional, basis. In this she was unexpectedly helped by the sentimental and chatty Madame Blanchard, who was so determined that she and Reid *were* a happy honeymoon couple that they were almost hypnotized into playing the part in detail.

Laintenon was too small a place for one not to run into anyone one knew from time to time. And it was only a few days before Leslie, out shopping one morning with Madame Blanchard, found herself face to face with Caroline in the small market-place.

They stopped, of course, and exchanged a few friendly words, though an atmosphere of mild hostility immediately wrapped Madame Blanchard around like a protective cloud. And when they had moved on again, she said to Leslie, in a hissing undertone,

"She is what you say 'no good,' that one."

"Oh, I wouldn't say that!" Leslie felt bound to protest — with some sincerity, as a matter of fact, because she was almost sure there was no real vice in Caroline. Only she could not help naturally attracting men. "She is here on her honeymoon too, you know."

Madame Blanchard seemed unnaturally surprised. But transparently relieved too.

"She is married now? So much the better. Though with some it makes no difference," she added rather darkly.

Leslie laughed. She could take Madame Blanchard's suspicions so much more easily than Reid's teasing.

"You're a little prejudiced, Madame, because she was engaged to your favourite, and then threw him over," she declared.

"You knew this, then?" Again Madame Blanchard was greatly surprised.

"Oh, certainly."

Leslie's companion muttered something to herself, but in such rapid and idiomatic French that Leslie found it impossible to follow. The general gist, however, seemed to be that the English were an extraordinary race, and quite unpredictable when it came to a question of the emotions.

This so genuinely amused Leslie that she could not resist adding teasingly,

"She married an old sweetheart of mine, as a matter of fact."

But this seemed to Madame Blanchard to border on the indecent. So, after a few protesting exclamations from her, they returned to the more normal topic of menus and supplies.

"Well, at least I've seen Caroline again, and managed to face the encounter calmly," Leslie told herself. "Being without Reid helped, of course. Perhaps if we don't all have to meet together again—— If Reid and I can leave here fairly soon—— If——"

That evening she broached the subject to him — casually and as though she had not thought much about it.

"How long do you think we shall be staying here, Reid?"

"Well——" he began, then he stopped and looked at her. "Do you want to go soon?"

"Not particularly. I just wondered."

"It's all taking longer than I expected," he confessed. "But I do feel that, now we're here, I'd better get the whole thing settled."

"Yes. Of course. There isn't anything I can do, is there? I don't mean with the lawyers. But perhaps in connection with the house. Sorting out things, and so on."

"Why, of course, if you like to. I thought you found the place melancholy."

"Oh — only in a rather sentimental way. It wouldn't depress me to be there alone, if that's what you mean. Anyway, the old caretaking couple are still there, aren't they?"

"Oh, certainly. Though they wouldn't be much company, I imagine. I should be in and out, of course. Or, if you liked, you could get Caroline to go along with you. She's unexpectedly efficient, when it comes to the point."

"I'm sure she is." Leslie hoped he didn't notice that her voice chilled a little. "But I'll try first on my own. She and Oliver will have their own affairs to attend to."

"No doubt," Reid agreed equably. And so it was arranged.

During the next few days, Leslie went each morning to the deserted villa outside the town and methodically dealt with each room in turn, deciding what should be kept, what should be sold and what might be given away.

She made lists for Reid to run through and approve or query at a later stage. And because she had plenty to do and less time to think, she was, on the whole, happier.

Each morning, as she approached the small white house where Oliver and Caroline were staying, she would feel her heart beat anxiously, in case she might have to stop and speak to one or other of them in the garden. But each morning she was spared this ordeal, and her heart-beats would subside again once she had passed the house and was safely on the stretch of road leading on to the Villa Rossignol.

So well and energetically did she work that, by the end of a week, she was able to tell Reid that she had dealt with all the principal rooms.

"Tomorrow I'll do what must have been a boudoir or personal sitting-room or something. It's quite small, but there's a great desk there, with all sorts of odds and ends, and one drawer at least full of correspondence," she told Reid.

"Is that so?" He looked both surprised and interested. "What sort of correspondence?"

"All mixed, I think — bills, receipts, personal letters and one or two books that look something like account books."

"I wonder——" began Reid, and then stopped.

"What do you wonder?" She smiled at him.

"Nothing. Something just came to my mind, but it's not important." He pushed back his chair and got up from the dinner table. "Look here, sweetheart, I'm sorry, but I'll have to leave you for this evening. There are still one or two things to attend to."

"Not the lawyers again, surely, at this time of night?" She looked surprised in her turn. "You certainly have them working overtime on Great-Aunt Tabitha's affairs. I should have thought the old lady could have left things a little straighter after ninety-odd years' experience of this wicked world."

"That's the trouble. She had time to make a lot of confusion in her ninety-odd years," Reid retorted lightly.

But he kissed her good-bye before he went — a thing he had not done since the evening she had told him to leave her alone — and she felt happier.

If he were returning to his habit of casually natural endearments that must mean that he felt they were more at ease with each other again.

When he had gone, she wrote a long letter home. Ever since they had come to Laintenon she had felt unable to write freely and happily as she had in Verona. Instead, she had contented herself with post-cards and the reiterated plea that she was very busy.

Now, with a sudden lightening of her heart, she felt that she could very well write to her mother, telling her all sorts of details about their life in Laintenon, her work at the villa and so on.

Once she had started, there seemed to be so much to say, and for over an hour Leslie wrote steadily.

Even when she had finished, there was still enough of the evening left to tempt her out of doors, and she decided to post her letter, and perhaps stroll up to the Villa. She had meant to bring Madame Blanchard some flowers from the lovely, overgrown garden that afternoon, but had forgotten them. This would be a good occasion to rectify the omission.

Slipping on a coat, for the evening air could be very chilly, but not bothering about a hat, she went out and, having posted her letter, started along the road to the Villa.

This time there was someone in the garden of the little house. As she came abreast of the gate, Oliver straightened up from some desultory weeding and came to lean his arms on the gate and greet her.

She stopped, to tell him where she was going and give him the latest news from home. And he volunteered, in his turn, the information that he and Caroline had just bought a car.

"Not a new one, or a particularly elegant one," he confessed. "But it will get us up and down to the coast. You and Reid must come along with us one day."

"It would be lovely," Leslie said, as sincerely as she could. "How is Caroline?"

"Blooming, as usual. She isn't in just now, otherwise she'd have come out to speak to you. She went off on some affairs of her own," Oliver explained, smiling indulgently. "Wouldn't tell me where she was going. She likes her little mysteries."

Leslie managed a creditable smile also.

"She'll probably arrive home with some special local dish for supper or something of the kind. Caroline is great on discovering things of that sort."

"Well, I hope it will be good," Leslie said politely. And went on her way.

When she reached the Villa, she went in by a side gate. She knew the grounds very well by now, and was quite clear about where to find the best flowers for Madame Blanchard.

They took some finding, because so much of the garden was overgrown now, but Leslie liked the half-wild appearance of the place, and she liked the atmosphere of deep solitude which the high stone walls induced.

She picked her flowers slowly and with enjoyment, arranging them with some care. And then, just as she selected the last few, the silence of the garden was broken by the sound of voices. Not the thin, rather wavering voices of the old people in charge of the house. But strong, laughing familiar voices.

Prompted by some instinct she could not have explained, Leslie drew behind a thick, overgrown hedge which hid her completely from sight. As she did so, Reid and Caroline came into view, walking along one of the more distant paths.

They were too far away for Leslie to hear what

they were saying, but they were both obviously in an excellent humour and laughing.

Then, even as she watched them with widened, angry eyes, they paused, evidently to say good-bye to each other.

Caroline put her hands on Reid's arms and said something which made him smile. Then she reached up and kissed him.

It was not a prolonged or passionate kiss. But it was a kiss. She went off towards the gate after that, and he turned and walked towards the house.

And even from where she was, Leslie could see that he was smiling in a very well-satisfied way.

CHAPTER TWELVE

LESLIE moved at last, because she realized that she was getting cold, but still she walked up and down some of the paths most distant from the house and tried to decide what she was going to do.

In the end, it was Reid who settled the question for her. He came out into the garden, having evidently seen her from one of the windows, and waved his hand and called to her.

"Hello! What brought you here?"

She came towards him until she was within easy speaking range. And then, because he seemed so unabashed, she knew she could not speak of what she had seen. *She* would be so ashamed for him. "I just looked in to get some flowers for Madame Blanchard. I meant to bring some home this afternoon. Have you been here long?"

"Yes. Most of the evening. I thought I'd like to have a look through those papers you mentioned."

Well, perhaps that was true!

"Did you find anything interesting?"

"Not what I was looking for."

"Were you looking for something special, then?"

"Not really." He was suddenly evasive. "I thought there might be something—— It doesn't matter. Have *you* been here long?"

There was nothing suspicious or anxious about his tone.

"No," she said coolly.

"Well, I'm ready to go home now, if you are."

"Yes, I'm ready," she said. And they left the place together.

As they approached Oliver and Caroline's place, Leslie saw that the discussed car was standing outside in the road, and both of them were hanging over it, presumably in ecstatic admiration.

"Hello," they all said, more or less together. And

Reid and Caroline, she noticed, showed no signs of having seen each other before during that evening.

"Come and look at the latest addition to our family," Caroline invited them.

And they too examined the finer points of the middle-aged car, and agreed that it was certainly capable of conveying one to the sea and back.

"Why don't we make a day of it tomorrow?" Caroline looked up, flushed a little from having been bent over the bonnet examining the car's interior. "The four of us, I mean. You don't *have* to shut yourself up in that stuffy lawyer's office every day, Reid, do you?"

"No. I don't have to."

"But it's as well to get things finished," Leslie cut in quickly.

"It's much better to seize on any good weather one can," countered Caroline promptly. "After all, you two are on your honeymoon too. It's going to be a wonderful day tomorrow. Look at that sky! Let's make a beach party, take our food and go down for the day."

"Sounds all right to me," said Oliver.

"To me too," Reid agreed.

They waited for Leslie's added agreement, as a foregone conclusion.

There was no objection she could raise — no argument she could oppose to this generally accepted idea of a party of pleasure. She made a virtue of necessity, smiled and said it was a wonderful idea. And everyone looked very well satisfied.

It was a matter of minutes to arrange the details. Oliver and Caroline undertook to call for the other two about ten the next morning, and each couple promised to bring a sufficient supply of food and drink.

"And swim-suits," Caroline added. "Down here the water will still be beautifully warm, and they say it's a wonderful shore."

"Not an entirely safe one, though," Reid said.

"There are some tricky under-currents. But we'll keep an eye on you girls."

"I like that! I'm a better swimmer than you are," boasted Caroline.

"Well, don't show off," her husband said, patting her dark head. "It isn't nice before company."

"Don't worry! I'll make her eat her words tomorrow," Reid declared gaily. And then he and Leslie went on their way.

She was very silent on the way home, and if Reid found that disturbing, she told herself, she could not help it.

If she had started to say anything beyond the merest conventional remarks, she would have found herself breaking into angry, frightened protests about the expedition on the morrow.

"And I must not have another of those outbursts," she told herself. "I *must not*. I should find myself upbraiding him for his meeting with Caroline tonight. I must be calm, and pleasant and unknowing. Oh, how I wish tomorrow were over!"

But tomorrow, like every other day since the world began, had to be lived through somehow, hour by hour.

She woke to a sense of indescribable foreboding, which the brightness of the day did nothing to dispel. And she thought, if it took so much effort to be reasonably bright at breakfast, what was it going to be like to pretend and pretend and pretend all day?

"I can't do it!" Leslie thought at one point.

And then, as though to give her a little strength and happiness to help her carry the burden of the day, the long-awaited miracle, which she had almost forgotten in her personal misery, actually happened.

Madame Blanchard came in carrying a telegram, and set it down before Leslie with an air of suppressed drama very suitable to the occasion.

"For me?" Leslie looked rather startled, and tore the envelope open.

The next moment she was crying aloud,

"Reid! Reid, come and look at this!"

And Reid, coming in from the next room, leant over her chair to read the message which trembled in her hand.

"Triumphant greetings," the telegram ran. "I salute you both — standing. Love and more thanks than I can say. — Morley."

"Oh, Morley! Darling, darling Morley!"

She began to cry excitedly — something of her pent-up feelings of the last few days going into those tears. And when Reid took her into his arms and stroked her hair, she clung to him, just as though he had never made secret assignations with Caroline or kissed her.

"There, honey, there!" He laughed very tenderly and kissed her. "There's nothing to cry about. It's wonderful news."

"That's why I'm crying," she sobbed, half laughing too. "Just because it *is* so wonderful and unbelievable."

"Well, I guess that's as good a reason as any for a few tears," Reid conceded with a laugh. And then, still holding Leslie, he turned to explain to Madame Blanchard, who had stood in the doorway during all this scene, divided between delight and dismay, and very much inclined to contribute a few tears herself.

Their landlady added her warm and most heartfelt congratulations, and advised them to waste no time in going off to celebrate the glad news with a day's pleasure.

As Caroline and Oliver arrived more or less at this moment, this seemed admirable advice. And, in the end, Leslie started off on the expedition with happier feelings and higher spirits than she would ever have thought possible an hour ago.

Oliver drove, of course, with Caroline sitting beside him, and contributing a little lazy advice from time to time. The other two sat behind and, because it seemed natural in their mood of shared excitement and relief, he held her hand rather tightly part of the time.

Once Caroline threw an amused, indulgent glance at them, and after that Leslie gently drew her hand away. But she had a warm little feeling at her heart because Reid's impulse had been to share her happiness, and what Caroline might think about it she really did not care.

Oliver was unfeignedly delighted at the news about Morley, and Caroline showed a pleasant degree of sympathy, considering that she knew so little of the background of the struggle which had preceded this triumphant achievement.

"I suppose you had been worrying a lot about your brother, although you didn't say much," she said to Leslie.

"Well, from time to time I did worry," Leslie admitted, remembering guiltily that sometimes, in the worry of her own affairs, she had momentarily almost forgotten Morley's. "Not that there was any likelihood of his being worse, you know. It was just that I knew what tremendously high hopes he had set on this experiment of Trevant's. It would have been so fearful for him if it had all been a failure."

"And you had been expecting the result almost any day?"

"I—— Yes, I knew it must be soon."

"I thought you seemed very depressed last night," Caroline said. "I suppose that was the trouble."

"No," Leslie replied levelly. "It was something else last night."

She felt Reid turn and glance at her. But Oliver said at that moment,

"Does anyone know this road? I think we went wrong about half a mile back."

The usual discussion followed, everyone holding a different opinion. And by the time they had discovered that they were on the right road, after all, Leslie guessed that no one would remember her remark.

She was wrong, however. Reid bent his head down to hers and said in an undertone,

"Was something wrong last night? What was the trouble?"

"Nothing I can talk about just now, Reid. Don't ask me now."

"All right. Will you tell me later?"

"Maybe."

She was not quite sure what had induced her to say that. Only, after the news about Morley, she had gathered a sort of inner courage. And, on the strength of that, she felt that perhaps it would be better to have the whole thing out with Reid. Quietly, of course, and without too much emotion. But so that at least everything was truthful and dignified between them.

The coast at this point was a beautiful one. Wild and rather rocky, but with a splendid stretch of golden sand when the tide was out, and it was not difficult to find the ideal place for a day-long picnic.

After they had taken all the things they needed out of the car, Oliver drove it a quarter of a mile into the tiny nearby village to park it safely, so that they need not worry about it while they swam or lounged on the shore all day.

It was a superb day, as Caroline had predicted, and as they were all more than reasonably good swimmers they spent a good deal of time in the water, only coming out to enjoy their excellent lunch.

Afterwards they lay on the sand, tossing an occasional remark to each other, but growing a little sleepy, if the truth be told.

Leslie, in fact, was just beginning to see the whole scene as a dim mist of blue and green and gold, when they were aroused by an urgent shout from a short, stout French official, who was climbing over the rocks with a purposeful air towards them.

"He can't be warning us off, surely? Isn't the seashore public property?" said Caroline, sitting up and rubbing her eyes.

"He's saying something about a car," replied Reid,

whose French was, naturally, a good deal more serviceable than that of the others.

Indeed, when the Frenchman, panting a little, had come right up to them, it was Reid who conducted the conversation from their side. Oliver, however, evidently caught enough to follow the general line, because at one point he shouted,

"What's that he says? Our car's been stolen?"

"No." Reid shook his head. "He says you stole it."

"Good lord! I like that. I've got the receipt for the damned thing. At least, I suppose I have."

He reached for his coat and began going through his pockets with some urgency.

"I don't think a receipt's going to help you much." Reid was attending still to the flow of talk from the purposeful official, but managed to slip in a word or two of explanation to the others from time to time. "He seems quite sure that it was stolen property — the thief didn't even bother to change the number plates — and if his story's true, you've been sold someone else's pup, old boy."

"But, look here——" Oliver had, to his own surprise, actually produced the receipt by now — "this means something, for the lord's sake! Tell him to get on to the fellow in Laintenon who sold me the thing."

"I think," Reid said, getting to his feet, "that you and I had better put a few clothes on and go along with this chap to the garage where the car is. We don't want the police collaring our only means of returning home."

"Need we both go?"

"Well, you're the owner, and perhaps I can do the explaining better."

"Yes, that's true. Will you girls be all right?" Oliver glanced at Caroline and Leslie.

"Yes, of course." They spoke simultaneously, and Leslie added, "We'll stay and look after everything here. You go along."

The two men threw on their coats and prepared to accompany the Frenchman.

"We shan't be long," Oliver promised optimistically.

But Reid, who had more experience of French small-town officialdom, said,

"Back tonight, I hope."

Leslie looked after them for a few minutes, and then dropped back on the sand.

She felt she did not want a long afternoon alone with Caroline, that the strain of making agreeable conversation would be more than she could stand, and, for a while at least, she was going to pretend to be sleepy.

Caroline fished a book out of their varied luggage, and seemed quite prepared to follow her own devices. Possibly, of course, she was no more anxious than Leslie for this prolonged *tête-à-tête*.

Overhead sea birds wheeled and called, and there was the ceaseless murmur of waves breaking on the shore. Otherwise there was silence and, after a while, Leslie's pretence at sleep gradually merged into the real thing.

When she woke up some time later, she was, to her surprise, alone. But, raising herself on her elbow and looking round, she saw that Caroline was swimming about leisurely quite close inshore.

Seeing Leslie sit up, she waved a hand and called, "Come on in. It's wonderful now."

Certainly the sea looked inviting, with the afternoon sun sparkling on the water. And unbuttoning the skirt of her beachdress, to reveal her slim green suit, Leslie ran down to the water's edge and waded out into the cream-edged, curling waves.

She swam near enough to Caroline to address a sociable word to her from time to time, but not near enough to feel that she was definitely in her company.

Presently she turned on her back and floated lazily, and revelled in the sensation of sun and sea.

"Race me to the tip of the promontory over there?" suggested Caroline amiably, swimming up alongside of her. "It's just about far enough for a warm afternoon."

Leslie didn't really want to bestir herself to that extent. But somehow a challenge from Caroline — even a challenge of this sort — was not to be refused. Besides — she was pretty sure she was the stronger swimmer.

"Right," she agreed, abandoning her pleasantly indolent floating. And a moment later they were travelling, neck and neck, towards the rather distant promontory.

"It's farther than she thought," reflected Leslie. And something sensible and reasonable in her warned her to suggest that they abandoned the attempt.

But Caroline was looking very fresh and going strongly. She was not, Leslie thought, in a mood to abandon any sort of competitive effort at this moment.

It was a perfectly friendly piece of rivalry, of course, proposed in genuine good-nature on Caroline's part. But, as the test lengthened and began to make real demands upon her, Leslie felt grimly that, in this as in the much more important matter, she and Caroline were real adversaries.

She must win. There was something symbolical about it. To fail would be to suffer a quite disproportionate loss of self-confidence. The failure in itself would not matter. It would be the fact that she had lost to *Caroline* which would rankle unbearably.

The distance really was much greater than she had imagined. And glancing over her shoulder at Caroline, who was a short length behind her, Leslie thought that she too had been disagreeably surprised by the amount of effort required to cover the distance.

Well, it was much too late to turn back now. They would have to go on, and allow themselves a considerable rest on that promontory before they attempted the journey back.

At the thought of having to cover this distance all over again, Leslie experienced a most unpleasant sinking of the heart. But she firmly reassured herself. They would feel better after a rest. And, anyway, the thing to concentrate upon at the moment was the journey out there.

As though in response to her common-sense determination, the difficulties seemed to ease slightly. She was travelling with less effort, and the rocky bulk of the promontory loomed very near now. With very little difficulty, she increased her speed, and shot ahead to victory in the last two minutes.

As she hauled herself out of the water, dripping and trembling rather with exertion, Caroline came up only a yard or two behind her. She too seemed to have found the last stretch less trying.

But she looked none the less anxious for that.

"You certainly made that in good time," she said, as she pulled herself up on to the rock beside Leslie. "But I don't like the implication of that last easy bit."

"You mean there was a strong under-current running with us?"

"Yes. And it will be against us going back."

Leslie turned her head suddenly and looked full at Caroline.

"I know. I'm thinking we're a couple of fools too. But we're strong swimmers, both of us. After a rest——"

"We can't afford a long rest," Caroline cut in shortly. "Look at that." She pointed to the stretch of water they had so recently covered.

Leslie stared at it for a long moment. At first, she thought it was her imagination which seemed to make it wider. Then she realized, with an uncomfortable thump of her heart, that there was no imagination about it. The tide was rising rapidly, and the distance between them and a safe shore was increasing every minute.

"At any rate the tide will be with us," she said steadily.

"Yes. But what about the pull of this darned underswell?" Caroline retorted. "We're in a nasty spot, Leslie. And I think, although we're tired, the sooner we try to get out of it, the better."

Leslie did not answer for a moment. She knew what Caroline was saying was horribly true. It was just a question of balancing between the length of time it would take to regain their strength, and the length of time it would take for the incoming tide to broaden that stretch of water beyond their fullest capacity.

"I think we'd better go," she agreed quietly.

And at that moment, to her inexpressible thankfulness, there appeared on the distant — terribly distant — shore where they had spent the morning, a figure. Only one figure. But, even at that distance, she knew it was Reid.

If they were to get into insuperable difficulties, he would be able to help them. No — one of them.

He was waving now, having evidently seen their bright, distinctive caps as they still clung to the rock, and his urgent gestures undoubtedly meant, "Hurry! Hurry!"

They probably, thought Leslie, with a wry gleam of humour as she struck out into the water again, meant, "Hurry, you unmitigated little idiots! Are you crazy, ever to have got yourselves into such a place?"

And then she didn't think any more humorous thoughts. Or, to tell the truth, of anything else at all but the terrible, overriding necessity of pitting her strength and skill against the remorseless "pull" of the water.

They kept close together this time, a little perhaps to encourage each other, but they wasted no effort on words.

Mentally, Leslie was counting to herself, very much as she had when she first learned swimming, because a rhythmical count seemed to help. But, beyond that, she tried not to think at all, because she had to concentrate, she told herself. She *had* to concentrate.

Once she raised herself slightly in the water and took a look at the distant shore. But she was so discouraged to find how comparatively little distance they had covered with such terrible effort that she decided not to look again.

Then she realized that her glimpse of the shore had shown it to be empty, and she knew, with a hopeful beat of her over-taxed heart, that Reid was on his way to help one of them.

Glancing to one side, she saw that Caroline too was still going strongly, but the effort was evidently telling on her equally. She was in quite as pressing need of help as Leslie herself.

In spite of her desire to concentrate on nothing but her swimming, Leslie's tired and harassed mind presented her suddenly with a completely clear picture.

There they were, the two of them, still struggling but with the odds most powerfully against them. Without assistance, it was doubtful if either of them would ever reach the shore and safety. Yet Reid could not hope to take on more than one of them.

"It's as simple as that," she thought, a great sob rising in her throat. "He can rescue only one of us. The one who matters more to him. And that is Caroline."

At that moment, Leslie very nearly gave up the struggle. But because the sheer will to live is probably the most powerful impulse in any human being, somehow she drove her exhausted body on through the water.

But she was going much more slowly now, and the effort seemed superhuman. Once a wave went over her head. She came up again, gasping and shuddering, and very, very frightened. And for the first time in all her life she really looked death in the face, and thought,

"It could really happen. If I get too tired to go on any more, it's over. I'll never see Mother's face again, nor lie in Reid's arms, nor feel the sun and the wind. The world will go on, but I shan't be there."

If only she could have been sure that she was safely on the incoming tide, she would have dared to float for a few minutes and rest. But she knew that, if she were not clear of that treacherous outgoing current, she might in a few moments lose half the distance she had gained, and she could never find the strength to recover it now.

"I can't — go on," she gasped once.

But no one heard her. And she went on. Endlessly, as it seemed.

All her life she must have been doing this. There had never been a time when she had not been struggling, in this fearful, heavy mechanical way.

She did not think of Caroline any more, nor even of Reid. She just went on and on and on and on.

CHAPTER THIRTEEN

AND THEN, at last, Leslie knew that she was finished. She would stop. It would be so much easier. She wondered she had not given in before, instead——

"All right, darling," Reid's voice said, not a couple of yards away from her. "Let yourself float. I can manage you."

Incredibly, the sound of his voice tore away the veils of illusion. There was still a life to be lived and a struggle to be made.

And there were other considerations too. Recollections which forced themselevs back on her with remorseless clarity.

"Caroline," she gasped. "She's — in danger — too."

"I can't manage more than one." His tone was grim and uncompromising.

"I know — understand." Mechanically, she was doing what he told her to do, but something in her urged her to protest. "That's why — you must — take her."

"Stop talking. My wife comes first."

She knew it was idiotic to waste words and breath now. But, though the effort brought the tears to her eyes, something greater than herself forced the final protest from her.

"No. She's — your love. She — comes first."

"You are my love and my wife," he said. "Now be quiet, for God's sake. We need our breath for something else."

She was quiet. Incredulously, rapturously, obediently quiet. She did exactly what he told her. She was even able to help herself a little, once his supporting arm had given her a tiny respite. In any case, the most difficult part of the journey was over.

But what gave her strength, far beyond any material consideration, was the fact that he had said she was his love.

The next few minutes were just a little vague. She was dimly aware that Reid was rubbing her vigorously with towels, wrapping her in a coat and making her drink brandy.

There were two or three other people there, she realized presently, and someone was sobbing breathlessly quite near her. With a dreadful feeling of guilt, she thought, "Caroline!" And though the effort hurt she rolled over on the sand to gaze in the direction of the sound.

It was a moment before she realized that the sobbing was not for Caroline, but from her. She was lying there, as exhausted as Leslie herself, and beside her knelt a dripping Oliver, his face a whitish-grey with anxiety and fear.

"She's safe too!" Leslie gasped, in a cracked little voice, and she felt the tears of hysteria rising in her also. "Reid——"

"Stop it!" Reid told her peremptorily. "Caroline will be as right as rain in an hour or two, and twice as dry. Don't you start crying, or probably Oliver and I will do the same. Come on, I'm taking you home now."

And he rolled her in a rug and lifted her in his arms.

One or two eager bystanders offered to carry her for him, seeing that he was a good deal exhausted already. But he would not let anyone else touch her.

Rather slowly, he carried her to the car which some kind passer-by had offered to put at their disposal. And still half dazed she was driven back to Laintenon, lying in Reid's arms, indescribably warmed by his tenderness and nearness, and possibly a little by the liberal amount of brandy he had poured down her throat.

She thought, "There are so many things to ask him and to tell him." But she could not think of the words in which to express any of them. And, since he seemed very well satisfied just to hold her and be silent, she felt that perhaps that was what she wanted too.

When they arrived at Madame Blanchard's, that good lady rushed out, with a natural premonition of disaster — or at least sensation — little short of miraculous. But though she exclaimed in a variety of keys and three different languages, she was intensely practical and helpful too. And in a remarkably short time Leslie had been undressed and put to bed with hot-water bottles.

The warmth and ease and quiet were so delicious after the ordeal through which she had gone that Leslie could not restrain one or two little groans of sheer relief.

Then, because it seemed the loveliest and the most natural thing in the world to do, she went to sleep, and bothered no more about anything or anyone for several hours.

When Leslie woke, the last of the golden evening light was filtering into the room, and she lay there loving it with the grateful tenderness which we attach only to a beautiful, familiar thing we have very nearly lost. She was alive when she might have been dead, and the world was a wonderful place.

Then a very slight movement beside her made her turn her head, and she saw, with a fresh rush of grateful tenderness, that Reid was lying back in the chair by her bed, quieter and more thoughtful than she usually saw him.

"Hello," she said softly. And he turned his head then and smiled at her.

"Hello, sweet. Feeling better?"

"I feel wonderful."

He leant forward, with his arm on the bed, so that he was very close to her.

"Promise me that you'll never take a risk like that again. I wouldn't relive this afternoon for all Great-Aunt Tabitha's fortune."

"I promise. I'm awfully sorry, Reid. It was very wrong and silly of us, I know. We started to race and — I felt I had to win. It seemed otherwise as though——"

"Yes?" he said, because she had stopped.

Her lashes came down, making shadows on her cheeks, and a very faint colour showed under her pale skin.

"Come on. Tell me," he coaxed, and kissed the side of her cheek softly.

"Reid — I thought you loved her."

"So I did," he retorted with cheerful candour. "Once."

"Oh, darling, I thought — as late as last night."

"Last night?" He looked mystified. "Why did you think I loved her last night, for heaven's sake?"

"Please don't think I was — was prying or suspicious or anything. But I came up to the Villa last night earlier than I told you, *really* just to get flowers for Madame Blanchard. And while I was there I saw you and Caroline laughing and talking together and she — she kissed you good-bye."

"Yes, that's true. She did," he agreed reflectively, as though recalling that with surprise.

"You had told me, Reid, that you had to go out and attend to some business affairs. I thought you meant you had to see the lawyers. And then — when I saw you with her in the garden——"

She broke off again, almost apologetically.

"Yes, I see. I'm sorry, my sweet. I wish I'd known. It was really a perfectly innocent meeting, you know. And quite unpremeditated on my part."

"Not on hers," she countered quickly.

"What makes you think that?" He twined his fingers loosely in hers and then raised her hand and kissed it lightly.

"I stopped to speak to Oliver on the way up — he was in their garden — and he remarked quite casually that she had gone out and refused to say where she was going. He thought it quite amusing, and was sure she was planning some small domestic surprise for him."

"Whereas you thought he was just being the blind husband?" Reid suggested, smiling.

"I didn't think anything about it until I saw her with you in the garden. Then I felt sure she had gone out on purpose to meet you."

"So far as it goes, that was true," Reid said slowly. "She saw me go past, up to the Villa, and she followed me because there was something she wanted to say to me."

"And what was that?" Leslie asked softly and quickly. "I mean — if it's not private and you can tell me."

"I can tell you, honey. Caroline has a passion for getting things straight, you know. Emotional situations, I mean. Probably it's because she has few inhibitions, and is naïvely interested in her own feelings. She wanted me to know — I believe for my own good as well as hers," he interjected with a dry smile, "that she was completely happy with Oliver and that she knew now that she had made a wise choice."

"She — said that?" gasped Leslie rather incredulously. "But why? I mean — why go out of her way to come and tell you that?"

"Because this visit of theirs to Laintenon had been in the nature of a test. On her part, I mean. I don't imagine Oliver knew anything of what was in her mind," Reid said, again with that smile. "She married him in a good deal of a hurry, remember. I guess she had her moments of doubt. It was not unlike her, you know, deliberately to come to this place which was full of — well, shall we say romantic memories of someone else? That was the final proof to her. If, in this place, she could still find Oliver the supreme attraction, then she'd know she had laid all the romantic ghosts of the past."

"She hadn't," Leslie said slowly, "reckoned on our being here too."

"Candidly, I think it added a zest to her own proof," Reid remarked with an air of reflective amusement.

"When she found that, even in the flesh, I no longer attracted her, although the scene was identical with the days when I had——"

"Didn't you any longer attract her?"

"Not to any degree that counted beside her Oliver," he confessed with a grin.

"I can't understand it," Leslie said with naïve simplicity. At which Reid laughed immoderately, but kissed her with great tenderness.

"Darling, is that how you see Oliver and me now? You never told me, you know."

"How could I?" She rubbed her cheek affectionately against his. "I thought you were still in love with Caroline."

"Yes, I see. You know, there's something to be said for Caroline's direct method. Having found that she loved only Oliver, she took quite a pleasure in letting me know that was the exact state of affairs. I'm not quite sure" — he rubbed his chin thoughtfully — "whether she thought I needed a final warning, or whether she just wanted to share her glorious discovery with someone else who knew a lot about her reactions."

"Reid——"

"Yes."

"What did you say, when she told you that?"

"If I remember exactly, I said, 'Thank God! Then there's no harm in telling you that I adore my wife and am supremely happy with her.' "

"You *really* — said that?"

"I did."

"Because, you know, I'd rather you told me the exact truth than — invented something to please me."

"There's no invention, my darling, about either the words or the sentiment. I do adore you and I am supremely happy with you," he said quietly. "Do you think you are such a difficult person to adore?"

"I don't know about that. I only know that I have always thought of you as being obsessed by a passion for Caroline."

He was silent for a few minutes. Then he said,

"When did you know you were no longer in love with Oliver?"

"Oh — after you and I decided to go on with the marriage in actual fact."

"And yet you had been very much in love with him for a long time before that, hadn't you?"

"Yes, I suppose" — rather reluctantly — "I had."

"You see, these changes can take place. I fell in love with you in Verona, and after that there could be no other woman for me. Neither Caroline nor anyone else. It isn't any stranger than your falling out of love with Oliver. Or, I suppose," he added reflectively, "Caroline falling out of love with me."

"That's the strangest of all," Leslie said, and was swept up in his arms and kissed several times.

"I shall hardly be able to let you out of my sight, after so nearly losing you," he declared.

"It wasn't such a bad thing, really, Reid." She was smiling brilliantly now. "It was the only thing that would have made me really convinced that you loved me better."

"Hell, why? I must say you girls think up some pretty gruelling tests."

She laughed outright then.

"Why, you see, I knew you could save only one of us. You *had* to make it the one you really loved."

He held her away from him and gave her a long, quizzical glance. Then he said,

"Darling, I just hate to undeceive you, and I hope this won't undermine your faith in my love for you. But I did know that Oliver was coming along a few yards behind me, and I should have reckoned in any case that his wife was his affair and my wife was mine."

"Oh," Leslie said very soberly. And then there was a long silence between them.

"Does it matter very much?" he asked at last, watching her serious face with loving and amused eyes.

"I think it does rather."

He took her right into his arms then and kissed her cheek and then her mouth.

"Do you really feel any doubt about my love for you?" he said. "Any doubts which could possibly be resolved by some swimming contest or artificial proof, I mean?"

She smiled slowly and pressed close against him.

"You think I'm very silly, don't you?" she said softly.

"Darling, I think everything about you is dear and lovely," he replied, with a gravity unusual in him. "But" — and his characteristic smile flashed out — "don't ask me to prove it with any trial by water. There are so many more interesting ways of doing it."

She laughed at that. A sweet, happy, relieved laugh.

"You don't have to prove it. I *know*," she said, and she felt her cares fall from her.

She lay there for a long while in the circle of his arm, both of them so happy and so much at one that there was hardly the need of words between them. Then she said lazily,

"Why did you go to the Villa yesterday evening?"

"What?" He roused himself. "Oh — I forgot. I went to look at those letters and account books you mentioned. You see, the old lady's lawyers were almost sure that she made all sorts of notes and tentative bequests before she actually settled on that final will, leaving everything to me. I thought if we could find some recent indication that she meant your father to have a good deal, he would accept what I'm making over to him with a better heart."

"Couldn't you have told me that," she said a little reproachfully, "and have let me help to look?"

"Oh — I guess it was silly of me. I wanted to find it for myself, and then bring it to you as a surprise."

"Reid! Who's the childish one now?" She put up her hand and touched his cheek lovingly. "And didn't you find anything, poor darling?"

"No. But there are still one or two things to look through. I hadn't time to finish."

She smiled at him indulgently, not knowing it was the first time she had ever felt sufficiently sure of him to do that.

"Do you want to go and complete the search now?"

"Not particularly."

"You can if you like." She gave a luxurious little yawn. "I'm getting sleepy again, anyway."

"All right." He held her for a moment longer, almost painfully tight. Then he kissed her and put her down.

At the door, he turned and smiled at her, so that she remembered the magic of those days in Verona and sensed all the magic of the days to come.

When he had gone, she lay there watching the last streak of the evening sun moving slowly across the opposite wall. She thought what a strange and wonderful day it had been. First the glorious news about Morley. Then the terrible struggle in the water. And finally the discovery that Reid loved her.

"It would be quite in keeping now for him to find that Great-Aunt Tabitha left Father half her money after all," she thought.

But that was a fanciful idea, and one which made her smile sleepily.

Anyway, it didn't really matter. For herself, she hardly cared at all who had the money. The only important thing about that inheritance was that, in leaving the money to Reid, Great-Aunt Tabitha had brought them together.

"Bless her, wherever she is!" thought Leslie. And, thinking that, she fell asleep again.

OMNIBUS — The **3 in 1** HARLEQUIN
only $1.75 per volume

Here is a great new exciting idea from Harlequin. THREE GREAT ROMANCES — complete and unabridged — BY THE SAME AUTHOR — in one deluxe paperback volume — for the unbelievably low price of only $1.75 per volume.

We have chosen some of the finest works of four world-famous authors . . .

SARA SEALE

JANE ARBOR

ANNE WEALE

ESSIE SUMMERS ②

. . . and reprinted them in the 3 in 1 Omnibus. Almost 600 pages of pure entertainment for just $1.75 each. A TRULY "JUMBO" READ!

These four Harlequin Omnibus volumes are now available. The following pages list the exciting novels by each author.

Climb aboard the Harlequin Omnibus now! The coupon below is provided for your convenience in ordering.

Sara Seale
Omnibus

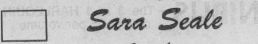

Her natural talent for creating the very finest in romantic fiction has been acknowledged and enjoyed by a great many readers since very early in Miss Seale's career. Here, we have chosen three perfect examples of her best loved and most cherished stories.

. . . . CONTAINING:

QUEEN OF HEARTS . . . when Selina presented herself to her new employer at Barn Close, the exclusive country hotel in Coney Combe, Devonshire, Max Savant had one thought, to send this "child" on her way. Now, it was impossible for him to imagine himself, or his hotel being without her. But, he must, for he has just become engaged to Val Proctor . . . (#1324).

PENNY PLAIN . . . at Plovers Farm, near the village of Chode, in England, Miss Emma Clay is employed as assistant and companion to the rather spoilt young lady, Mariam Mills. Their relationship proves to be rather stormy, not the least cause of which is the country vet, in his country tweeds, the uncompromising Max Grainger . . . (#1197).

GREEN GIRL . . . Harriet listened to the incredible suggestion that she marry this total stranger and thus solve her dilemma, and the trouble which he himself was in. Whilst she knew full well that her own plight was quite hopeless, instinct warned her that Duff Lonnegan's trouble was far more serious than even he knew . . . (#1045).

$1.75 per volume

Jane Arbor
Omnibus

Jane Arbor chooses inspiring locations, peopled with the most life-like characters, — then inter weaves her gripping narratives. Her achievements have brought her world renown as a distinguished author of romantic fiction.

· · · · · · · · · · CONTAINING:

A GIRL NAMED SMITH . . . Mary Smith, a most uninspiring name, a mouselike personality and a decidedly unglamorous appearance. That was how Mary saw herself. If this description had fitted, it would have been a great pleasure to the scheming Leonie Crispin, and could have avoided a great deal of misunderstanding between Mary, Leonie and the handsomely attractive Clive Derwent . . . (#1000).

KINGFISHER TIDE . . . Rose Drake was about to realize her most cherished dream' — to return to the small village of Maurinaire, France. To manage her aunt's boutique shop produced grand illusions for Rose, but from the very day of her arrival, they were turned to dismay. The man responsible was the town's chief landowner and seigneur, a tyrant — living back in the days of feudalism . . . (#950).

THE CYPRESS GARDEN . . . at the Villa Fontana in the Albano Hills in Italy, the young, pretty Alessandra Rhode is subjected to a cruel deception which creates enormous complications in her life. The two handsome brothers who participate come to pay dearly for their deceit — particularly, the one who falls in love . . . (#1336).

$1.75 per volume

Anne Weale

Omnibus

The magic which is produced from the pen of this famous writer is quite unique. Her style of narrative and the authenticity of her stories afford her readers unlimited pleasure in each of her very fine novels.

. . . . CONTAINING:

THE SEA WAIF . . . it couldn't be, could it? Sara Winchester the beautiful and talented singer stood motionless gazing at the painting in the gallery window. As she tried to focus through her tears, her thoughts went racing back to her sixteenth birthday, almost six years ago, and the first time she set eyes on the sleek black-hulled sloop "Sea Wolf", and its owner, Jonathon "Joe" Logan . . . (#1123).

THE FEAST OF SARA . . . as Joceline read and re-read the almost desperate letter just received from cousin Camilla in France, pleading with Joceline to come and be with her, she sensed that something was terribly wrong. Immediately, she prepares to leave for France, filled with misgivings; afraid of learning the reason for her cousin's frantic plea . . . (#1007).

DOCTOR IN MALAYA . . . Andrea Fleming desperately wanted to accompany the film crew on the expedition, but Doctor James Ferguson adamantly refused stating that if she went along, he would refuse to guide them. But, Guy Ramsey had other ideas, and cunningly devised a scheme whereby Andrea would join them — in a manner which the Doctor could not oppose . . . (#914).

$1.75 per volume

Essie Summers ②

Omnibus

Without doubt, Miss Summers has become the first lady among those who write of the joy and splendour of romance. Her frequent use of locations in New Zealand, the country of her birth, has a timeless appeal to her readers throughout the world.

. . . . CONTAINING:

HIS SERENE MISS SMITH . . . she was very certain that never again, under any circumstances would she ever become involved with a member of the male management of any firm where she was employed. Then, William Durbridge came thundering into her life, and before long, was making his way straight to her heart . . . (#1093).

THE MASTER OF TAWHAI . . . Tawhai Hills Estate lay deep in the green rolling country of South Canterbury, New Zealand. It was here that the wealthy young Rowena Fotheringham came to work in the hope of being accepted for herself — not her fortune. She could easily have been, had she not decided to deceive the very first man who had ever really cared for her, complicating both their lives . . . (#910).

A PLACE CALLED PARADISE . . . no one must ever know the truth, the reason why Annabel Lee had come to Paradise, an isolated plateau at the head of Lake Wakatipu in New Zealand. She did not know how deeply she would come to love a man called Gideon Darroch, nor how it would affect him — if he learned her secret . . . (#1156).

$1.75 per volume